THE GUNSMITH

467

The Lady Sheriff

Books by J.R. Roberts
(Robert J. Randisi)

The Gunsmith series

Gunsmith Giant series

Lady Gunsmith series

Angel Eyes series

Tracker series

Mountain Jack Pike series

COMING SOON!
The Gunsmith
468 – Death in the Family

For more information visit:
www.SpeakingVolumes.us

THE GUNSMITH

467

The Lady Sheriff

J.R. Roberts

SPEAKING VOLUMES, LLC
NAPLES, FLORIDA
2021

The Lady Sheriff

ISBN 978-1-64540-409-5

Chapter One

Pleasant, Wyoming did everything it could to live up to its name.

For Clint it started with the livery stable. The hostler there probably had the nicest personality he'd ever run into at a stable.

"Nice ta see ya, stranger," the big man said. "What can I do fer ya?"

"I just want to board my horse for a day or two," Clint told him.

"A day or two?" the man asked. "Yer gonna wanna stay here longer than that. This here's a right nice town, with nice people. The name ain't just a name, ya know. We like ta live up to it."

"I can see that," Clint said, "but let's start with a day or two and see where that leads."

"I tell ya what," the man said, accepting the Tobiano's reigns, "if ya wanna stay a third day, I'll make that one on the house."

"That's real nice of you," Clint said.

"This is a fine lookin' animal," the man said. "I'll take good care of 'im."

"Have you got a suggestion for a hotel?" Clint asked.

"We got two," the man answered, "and they'll both do right by ya."

"That's good to know. Thanks."

He grabbed his saddlebags and rifle and left the livery.

The first hotel he came to said THE GRAND HOUSE HOTEL above the door. He stepped into the lobby, found it neat, clean and empty but for the front desk, a clerk, and a brown divan against one wall. Off to the right was a stairway leading up.

The clerk was in his thirties and had a huge, beaming smile.

"Good-afternoon, sir," he said, as soon as Clint stepped through the door. "Can I help you?"

"Yes," Clint said, "I need a room."

"Of course," the man said. "And for how long?"

"Oh, a night or two."

"Really?" the clerk asked. "You're going to want to stay longer than that, sir."

"So the man at the livery told me," Clint said. "Let's start with two nights."

"Whatever you say, sir." The clerk turned the register so Clint could sign and plucked a key from the board behind him. Then he turned the book around so he could read what Clint wrote.

"Mr. Adams," he said, "welcome." He held the key out. "Room two, top of the stairs."

That suited Clint, because he knew the room would not overlook the street.

"Thank you."

He went up the stairs to room two and let himself in. It was small, but very clean. It had everything he'd need for his stay: a bed, a chest of drawers he probably wouldn't use, a pitcher-and-basin on a small table against the wall with a mirror on it that he could use to shave. He put his rifle and saddlebags on the bed and left the room.

In the lobby he asked the clerk, "Where can I get a good steak?"

"We have a dining room," the clerk said, "but we only serve breakfast. However, just across the street you'll find Hattie's Café. She's a wonderful cook."

"Thanks."

Clint walked out the front door and immediately saw Hattie's across the street. It was hard to miss, with the name in red above the door. He crossed over and entered.

"Well, hello there," a heavyset, grey-haired woman with a beautiful smile greeted him. "Can I get you a table, stranger?"

"Yes, thank you," he said. "Something in the back?"

"The back?" she said. "I have a very nice table by the window, so you can look out at our beautiful town."

"No, that's all right," he said. "I'll just take a table in the back."

"Whatever you want," she said. "This way."

As she showed him to a table in the back, they walked between other occupied tables. Whether there was a family, a couple, or a man or woman alone, they all looked up at Clint, nodded their heads and smiled.

"Have you just arrived in our town?" she asked, as Clint sat.

"Yes, moments ago, actually."

"Then you're tired and hungry."

"Yes."

"Coffee?"

"Please, and a steak?"

"A steak dinner, coming up," she said. "My name's Hattie, by the way. I'm the owner, and the cook."

"And the waitress, apparently."

"Oh, just for today," she said. "My regular waitress is home, ill. But she'll be back tomorrow."

"That's good."

"I'll get your meal," she said, and hurried away.

Chapter Two

Clint was used to being stared at. What he wasn't used to was having it done with such smiles. Everyone in the place seemed too happy, so . . . pleasant.

Hattie brought Clint his coffee, and then a plate with a perfectly cooked steak smothered in accompanying vegetables.

"Tell me something Hattie," he said.

"Yes?"

"What makes everyone in this town so . . . happy?"

"There's no reason not to be happy," she said. "We have everything we want, here. Our businesses are thriving."

"How long has the town been called Pleasant?" he asked.

"Not long," she said. "Not even a year."

"And has it been during that time that this . . . happiness has come into your lives?"

"Why yes, I believe it has," she said. "Excuse me, I have others to attend to. Please, enjoy your meal."

He did. The steak was perfectly cooked, the potatoes and carrots almost melted in his mouth. He had to admit, he was pretty happy himself since arriving in Pleasant. But it was an odd place . . .

***

After he finished eating, he paid his bill and thanked Hattie for the wonderful meal.

"You see?" she said. "Even you have a smile on your face as you leave here."

"That's because of your food," Clint said.

"What brings you to this town, anyway?" she asked.

"Just passing through," he said. "I never heard of it, so I thought I'd have a look."

"I have to be back to work," she said, "but take a long look. You might like what you see."

She turned and went back to the kitchen, while he stepped outside. People passing nodded to him and smiled, and he nodded back. There were no raised voices on the street, no one was arguing. He wondered how it would be in the saloons later, when men were drinking and gambling? But that wouldn't be for a while.

He decided to take a walk around town, see if he could find an area where the people might not be smiling so much. But he walked the length of the main street, and back again, and didn't see one frown. He did, however, see the town's three saloons, and decided to stop into one. It was called The Moon Shadow Saloon.

As he went through the doors, he saw there were about half a dozen men inside, three at the bar, and three seated at tables. The bartender looked over at him and smiled as he approached.

"Stranger in town," he said. "Welcome."

"Thanks."

"What can I getcha?"

"A beer."

"What brings you to Pleasant, stranger?" one of the men at the bar asked.

"I'm just passing through, friend," Clint said. "Never heard of the town, so I thought I'd have a look."

"Never heard of it because it used to be called West Fork," the man said. "Got changed about a year ago."

Clint accepted the beer from the smiling bartender, but noticed that the three men standing at the bar weren't smiling.

"By who?" Clint asked.

"The new Mayor and his crew."

"His crew?"

"His City Council."

Clint sipped his beer then put it down.

"I've been here a couple of hours now," he said. "Checked into the hotel, put my horse up at the livery, had a steak at Hattie's . . . you fellas are the first ones I've seen who aren't smiling."

"We don't live in town," the spokesman said. "We work out at the Big Fork ranch."

"Big Fork?" Clint asked. "Any relation to the old name of the town?"

"Yeah," the man said, "for some reason Mr. Caldwell likes the word Fork. It used to be the biggest spread in the county."

"Not anymore?"

"It's been cut into pieces, and the pieces sold off," the man said.

"Collins—" the bartender started.

"Naw, naw, Benny," Collins said, "he's new in town. Let's fill 'im in."

"That ain't a good idea," one of the men seated at a table chimed in.

"Then maybe it ain't a good idea for you to be here, Ned," Collins said.

Collins was a fit man in his thirties, like his two friends. They were probably good ranch hands.

The man called Ned was sitting alone at a table. The other occupied table had two men, who smiled at Clint when he walked in. Now Ned stood up, dropping the smile he'd been wearing.

"I guess I better go," he said. "You boys comin'?" He stood up, revealing himself to be well over six feet, but mostly skin and bones.

The other two men stood up and followed Ned out.

"Where was I?" Collins asked.

"You were going to fill me in," Clint said, "but why don't I buy you boys a drink before we do that?"

Chapter Three

Clint had beers set up in front of each man, and then the bartender stood back and folded his arms. He was in his fifties, with a white apron wrapped around his girth.

"Why do you want to fill me in, Mr. Collins?" Clint asked.

"Just Collins," the man said. "Nobody calls me Mister. And this is Pete and Sam."

"My name's Clint."

"Well, Clint, you're a stranger, and to tell you the truth, this town don't get many strangers."

"The mayor's tryin' to change that, too," the bartender spoke up. "He's tryin' to get a stageline in here."

"Yeah, well, that'll take a while," Collins said to the bartender, then looked at Clint again. "My boss founded the town of West Fork, built it up over a twenty-year period, but he got stuck. Couldn't get us a bank or a stageline. That's when Frank Westin stepped in."

"He's the Mayor?"

Collins nodded.

"He got himself elected with lots of promises and took over. Took the town away from my boss. Preached the only way this town was gonna grow was to change the name and everybody's attitude along with it. So the town became Pleasant, and now everybody smiles."

Clint looked at the bartender, who just shrugged.

"Seems like the mayor is doing a pretty good job of keeping his people happy, then," Clint commented.

"Some people," Collins said. "Not my boss."

"What's your boss' name?"

"Lawrence Crandall."

"Never heard of him," Clint said.

"That's a shame," Collins said. "He used to be a big man in these parts."

Clint finished his beer.

"Well, thanks for the information."

"You wanna stay around here for a while," Collins said, "just remember to smile."

Clint was turning to leave when something occurred to him.

"You got law here?" he asked.

"Sorta," Collins said.

"What's that mean?"

Now the three men did smile, and Collins said, "You'll see."

Clint let it go and left the saloon.

***

After Clint left the Moon Shadow, Collins turned to Pete, Sam and Benny.

"I think we got our man," he said.

"Why?" Pete asked. "He's a stranger."

"That's why," Collins said. "We've been waitin' for a stranger."

"He don't look like easy pickins to me," Benny the bartender said.

"That makes him even better," Collins said. "There's no reason the people in town won't believe that he was the one."

"So when do we move?" Pete asked.

"Soon," Collins said. "Let's see how long he's stayin'."

"And who he is," Benny added.

Collins looked at the older man and nodded.

***

Clint decided to go back to his hotel and come out later in the evening to see how the saloons were then. He sat on the bed and took a book from his saddlebags, a collection of his friend Mark Twain's stories. He'd been going through it slowly.

He was about to open the book when there was a knock. Setting the book aside he drew his gun and went to the door.

"Who is it?"

"The sheriff," a woman's voice said.

He opened the door and looked out, expecting to see a man and a woman. All he saw was a woman, and she was wearing a badge. He opened the door.

"You mind if we talk?" she asked.

"About what?"

"You're a stranger," she said. "I keep track of the strangers who come to town."

"I've been told you don't get many."

"That's pretty true, but all the more reason I check."

"And you're the sheriff?"

"That's right. Sheriff Holliday."

"Holliday?"

"That's my name."

"I'm sorry," he said, "but I don't know of many towns hiring women to be their sheriffs, these days."

"Well," she said, "nobody else wanted the job. What can I say? Now, do you mind if I come in, Mr. Adams?"

She knew who he was, which also explained the visit.

"Come on in, Sheriff," he said.

Chapter Four

"You won't need that," she said, gesturing to his gun. "I mean, I know you're the Gunsmith, but I'm just here to talk."

She was dressed like a man, right down to the gunbelt around her waist that hung low on her left hip. She was blonde, tall, solidly built, in her thirties, and not the least bit intimidated by him.

Clint holstered his gun.

"You always wear your gun in your room?" she asked.

"I'll be going out again in a while, or I would've hung it on the bedpost."

"Ah." She nodded, stood right where she was, in front of the closed door.

"Would you like to sit?" he asked. "I have nothing to offer you."

"I tell you what," she said. "This hotel has a small dining room they use for breakfast. We can go there to talk, and I think I could convince them to bring us some coffee."

"That suits me," he said.

"Good! Shall we go?"

They left the room and headed down to the lobby.

"How long have you been sheriff?" Clint asked, as they walked.

"Several months, now."

"Any deputies?"

"Nope."

"Why not?"

"Do you know any men who want be a deputy under a female sheriff?" she asked.

"Good point."

The clerk watched as they walked across the lobby.

"I assume he told you I was here?" Clint nodded toward the clerk.

"Both hotels keep me informed when a stranger checks in," she confirmed.

When they reached the dining room, the sheriff went into the kitchen, then came out and told Clint, "They'll bring the coffee. I assume you'll want to sit away from the windows."

"That's right."

"Let's go to the wall, over there."

They sat at a table, with a wall to his right and the rest of the room to their left. A small, older woman came out of the kitchen and walked quickly to their table with a coffee pot and two cups. She was smiling the whole way.

"Thanks, Edna," the sheriff said.

"You're very welcome, Sheriff."

Edna went back to the kitchen. Clint grabbed the pot and poured two cups.

"Thank you," she said.

"I'm assuming you're going to ask me why I'm in your town," he said.

"You've played this scene before," she replied.

"Many times. I'll tell you what I told everyone else," he said. "I'm passing through."

"Everybody else?"

"The hostler at the livery, the clerk at the hotel and the bartender in the saloon."

"Which saloon?"

"The Moon Shadow."

"That'd be Benny," she said.

"We didn't introduce ourselves."

"Anybody else in there?" she asked.

"Six men," Clint said. "I talked to three while the other three left."

"You remember who you talked with?"

He hesitated, then said, "Collins, Pete and Sam. Collins did all the talking."

"He would."

"They told me they were ranch hands."

"They are, now," she said. "Before that they were bank robbers."

"How'd they get jobs on the ranch?" he asked.

"Lawrence Crandall hired them," she said. "At the time he was trying to buy as many guns as he could."

"What happened?"

"He didn't get enough," she said. "He wanted to ride in here and take the town back, but he didn't have enough men. After that Mayor Westin started to take slices of his land and give it to others to homestead."

"So they appreciated it, and they back him."

"Right."

"And I assume it's not only the people who live in Pleasant who are happy, but some who live on the outskirts."

She nodded.

"Mayor Westin ran unopposed the next election," she said, "and he will again."

"Is he the one who gave you your job?"

"He did," she said, "but he did it as a joke."

Clint sat back and stared at Sheriff Holliday.

"Why do I have the feeling the joke's on him," he said.

"He didn't think I'd act like a real sheriff, but I have," Holliday said. "And I always will. That's why we're here." She leaned forward in her chair. "I need you to leave town."

Chapter Five

"Why?"

"You're the Gunsmith," she said. "I don't need that kind of trouble here."

"You think I'm a threat to all the smiling faces here?" he asked.

"I don't know," she said. "Are you?"

"I told you I was just passing through," Clint said. "I want one more day of rest for my horse, and then I'll leave."

"One more day?"

"Let my horse rest today and tomorrow, and I'll leave the next morning."

"That sounds fair," she said.

"I'm not looking for trouble," he said. "Is there anybody in this town who might come looking for me?"

"Not any of the townspeople."

"What about Collins and his people?" Clint asked. "Will they be tempted?"

"They might," Sheriff Holliday said. "If they're still in town, I'll have to keep an eye on them."

"That'll make two of us."

***

After coffee they both stepped outside the hotel.

"What was the real reason you wanted to talk to me?" he asked.

"What makes you think asking you to leave wasn't the reason?" she asked.

"Like I said," he replied, "I told everybody I was only here for a day or two. So you already knew I was leaving."

"Maybe I just didn't want the Gunsmith to think I was a joke," she said.

"Well you succeeded," Clint said. "Thanks for the coffee, Sheriff Holliday."

"You're welcome."

Holliday walked away from the hotel, looking for all the world like anything but a joke. Clint had the feeling she could handle the gun she was wearing.

He turned and went back inside to Mr. Twain.

***

The other two saloons in town were called The Grand, and the Hanging Man. Of the three, the one he had visited that afternoon—the Moon Shadow—

appeared to be the smallest. He decided this time to try the largest.

He approached the Grand Saloon and stood out front for a few moments, taking in the cacophony of noise coming from within. There were raised voices, laughter, music and so much bright light inside that it seemed to add to the sound.

He entered and actually had to squint against the brilliance coming from the crystal lamps in the ceiling. The smiling faces turned to look at him, but then went back to talking and laughing with each other.

Clint approached the bar, where a smiling bartender in his early thirties greeted him.

"Welcome to the Grand Saloon," he said. "Whiskey, beer. Gambling or . . . company?"

"Let's start with a beer and go from there," Clint said.

"Cold one comin' up," the man said.

When the bartender set the mug down, there was sweat running down the sides. Clint picked up the beer and turned his back to the bar. There were several house games going on, and the dealers in each case seemed to be women wearing plunging gowns. Probably to balance them off, the saloon girls working the floors all had skirts that were showing off their ankles and legs.

The games were Faro, Poker and Blackjack.

Poker was Clint's preference, but he liked private games over house games. The house took too much of a cut for his liking.

He didn't like blackjack at all. The house drew way too many twenty-ones to beat his twenty over the years, so he stopped playing a long time ago.

Faro was his friend Wyatt Earp's game, but one that never appealed to Clint.

As he looked around, the crowd seemed to be made up of a variety of customers. He saw ranch hands, shopkeepers, townsmen in suits. Unless they were seated at one of the gaming tables, the groups seemed to be keeping to their own.

Clint eyed a group of men in suits and wondered how many of them were businessmen on the town council? And he wondered if the mayor, himself, was in attendance.

He finished his cold beer and set the empty mug down on the bar.

"Another?" the bartender asked.

"No, thanks," Clint said. "Maybe another time."

"Come on back," the man said.

Clint nodded, left the Grand Saloon and headed for the Hanging Man.

Chapter Six

The Hanging Man was almost the opposite of the Grand. The sign over the door had the name of the place and the outline of a hanging man. There was no music coming from inside and no bright light. However, there were still loud voices and laughter. When he entered, he saw the gaming tables immediately, as they were lined up in front. There was a wheel of fortune as well as roulette, so the air was filled with the spinning sound of either wheel.

He approached the bar, which was crowded with customers both drinking and laughing. But so far, in three casinos, he hadn't seen one fight, or heard one argument.

He had never before been in a town where it seemed to be against the law to be unhappy.

He managed to elbow his way to the bar and order a beer from the busy, happy bartender.

"Ain't never seen you before," the bartender said, as he served him.

"Just rode in today."

"Thought so," the man said. "First one's on the house to strangers."

"Thanks."

As he did in the Grand, he turned his back to the bar with his beer in hand and looked the place over. He actually preferred the Hanging Man. The light in the place wasn't as bright, and he liked the sound of the roulette ball bouncing around on the wheel.

He was finishing up his beer and about to leave to head for the Moon Shadow when the batwing doors opened, and sheriff Holliday came in.

He watched as the men in the place turned to look at her. Because he was watching closely, he saw some smiles slip. They all stared as she started for the bar.

"Buy you a drink, Sheriff?" he asked.

"Why not? Nobody else in here will."

"Why's that?" he asked.

"Unlike you," she said, "they still think I'm a joke."

"How do you intend to convince them you're not?"

"I haven't worked that out, yet."

Clint and Holliday turned to the bar, and Clint signaled to the bartender for two beers.

"I come in here during my rounds," she said. "Usually, I don't have a drink."

"Well, I'm here to buy it for you," he said, as the bartender set the beers down. "If they don't like it, too bad."

"Oh, they don't mind if I drink," she said. "They just don't want me acting like a real sheriff."

"Have any of them given you a reason to?"

"Not yet," she said, "but it's coming. One of these days, somebody's going to want to test me. The way men are always testing you."

"I don't wish that on anyone," he said.

She turned her head to look at him.

"I was a teacher," she said, "until the people here stopped sending their children to school."

"Why'd they do that?"

"It made their children happy to stay home," she said. "That's what they wanted, happy, smiling children."

"That doesn't sound right."

"That's why I took the sheriff's job," she said. "If I couldn't help as a teacher, I thought I might be able to help as the law. But so far, they won't let me."

"It says a lot about you that you're still here," he said, "and still wearing that badge."

"Might mean I'm a fool," she said.

"It might," he agreed, "but I don't think so." He turned and looked around. "I was over at the Grand before I came here. Is it always like that?"

"Pretty much," she said. "Everybody comes out at night to have a good time."

"And are they at work in the morning?"

"Pretty much."

"Then I guess I can't criticize their lifestyle, if it's working."

She sipped her beer.

He turned back and looked at her.

"It is working, isn't it?"

"For most of them, I guess."

"But not for you."

She shrugged.

"What does it matter if it's not working for one person?" she asked.

"I guess that remains to be seen," Clint said.

***

"He's at the Hanging Man," Pete said.

"Good," Collins said. "That place is so crowded nobody will remember if he was there or not. Where's Sam?"

"He's waitin' right outside," Pete said. "Collins, you really think this'll work?"

"It'll work," Collins said. "Let's go."

Chapter Seven

Mayor Frank Westin had two major goals in mind for the town of Pleasant. One, he wanted to open the Pleasant Bank, and two, he wanted to get a stageline to not only stop in town but open a station.

For the time being, he had the town's funds in the private safe in his office, along with a book that listed all the names of the depositors and their balances. Once he had the bank up and running, the money would be transferred.

As for the stageline, he was in contact with three different ones. Since Pleasant did not have a telegraph line, he would travel to the next town—Bridgeton—and use theirs. Sometimes he would send someone there to retrieve or send messages.

A telegraph line for the town would have to come later.

He put the book in the large, cast iron, security safe and closed the door. It was four feet tall and three feet square. He'd had it shipped in from Kyser & Rex in Frankfurt, Pennsylvania.

Once he was sure it was closed nice and tight, he left his office and headed for his house, which was on the outskirts of town.

***

Collins, Pete and Sam stopped across the street from the City Hall building.

"Are we goin' in?" Pete asked.

"Wait," Collins said. "He always leaves late."

It was dark. The town didn't have lights on the street, yet. Eventually, the front door opened, and a figure came out.

"That's him," Collins said.

"You sure?" Sam asked.

"Who else would it be?" Collins asked. "Besides, see that slight limp? That's our mayor."

They watched as the figure walked off down the street.

"Let's go," Pete said.

"Wait," Collins said. "Let him get further away. There's no rush."

Collins relaxed against the outer wall of the hardware store. Pete and Sam were restless.

"Collins?" Pete said.

"Yeah, okay," Collins said, "let's move."

They trotted across the street to the front door of City Hall. It was locked, but that didn't stop them. Sam jimmied the door open, and they went inside.

"The Mayor's office," Collins said, "That's where the safe is."

They went up the stairs to the second level and found Mayor Westin's office. They stopped just inside the door and stared at the safe across the room.

"There it is, Pete," Collins said. "Can you open it?"

"Luckily," Pete Selby said, "it's an old Kyser and Rex. Just watch me."

He walked to the four-foot safe and knelt down.

"I'll need some light," he said.

"They'll see a light from outside," Sam complained.

"Sam, you stand between us at the window. I'll light a match."

While Sam did as he was told, Collins lit a match, shielded it with his hand, and held it to the front of the safe. Pete was able to work, and before long he had the safe open.

Collins had saddlebags over his shoulder. They proceeded to fill them with money.

"No gold?" Sam complained.

"It woulda been too heavy to carry, anyway."

When they were done, the saddlebags stuffed, they were bulging. Collins tossed them back over his shoulder.

"Let's get outta here," he said.

"Wait a minute," Sam said. "How do we pin this on the Gunsmith?"

"He gets to town and right away there's a robbery?" Collins said. "Also, there's gonna be a witness who saw him prowling around City Hall tonight."

"What witness?" Pete asked.

Collins looked at Sam Tennant.

***

Sheriff Holliday looked around, then set her empty mug down on the bar.

"I'm going to head back to my office," she said.

"Not going home?" Clint asked.

She smiled.

"The office is my home. I sleep in one of the cells."

"The town doesn't supply you with a place to live?" he asked.

"You forget," she said, "the town doesn't take me seriously. What about you? Had enough of this, yet?"

"I might stop in at the Moon Shadow," Clint said.

"That'll be a quiet place for you to drink," she told him. "Don't forget your promise."

"I rest my horse tomorrow, and I'm gone the next morning, Sheriff. But I just got an idea."

"What's that?"

"Why don't we let the whole town see you escorting me out?" he suggested.

"I'm just not a game player, Mr. Adams," she said. "Good-night."

He watched her walk out without a glance behind her. He admired her resolve, but thought if this was any other kind of town, she'd never last.

Chapter Eight

The first thing Mayor Westin saw when he entered his office the next morning was the open door of his safe.

"Sonofabitch!" he swore. He rushed to it and saw that all the money was gone. "*Son*ofabitch!"

He called an emergency meeting of the Town Council, by going out and fetching each member himself.

***

"Too bad we don't have a real lawman," Neil Lomax, the owner of the mercantile, complained.

"I told you," the Mayor said, "I'm working on that, too."

"Yeah," Lomax said, "but we could use one now!"

"Look," the Mayor said, "I don't need criticism, I need suggestions."

"Well," Harve Bennett, owner of the feed store, said, "we've got a badge-toter, we might as well use her."

"Get serious!" the Mayor said.

"Hey," Bennett said, "you gave her the badge."

"Only because nobody else wanted it," Mayor Westin said. "This kind of thing isn't supposed to happen in this town."

"Why not?" Lomax asked. "Just because you renamed it Pleasant?"

"We've been tellin' you," said the third member of the council, Sid Williams, owner of the leather shop, "you got things in the wrong order. You shoulda got us a real lawman first, then worry about a bank, and a stage-line."

"And," said the fourth member, owner of the Grand Saloon, Dan Hawkins, "let everybody hold onto their own money until we *did* have a bank, instead of keepin' it all in your safe."

Westin stared back at the four men, all of whom were watching him, warily.

"Are you sayin' you think I took the money?" he asked, finally.

"Hey," Hawkins said, "I'm just sayin', your safe, your office."

"Okay, hold on," Lomax said, waving his hands, "we're not saying you took the money. But you didn't do much to safeguard it."

"We just think your priorities have been in the wrong order," Williams said.

"Everybody in this town has gone along with me up to now," Westin pointed out.

"That's because so far everything's gone the way you said it would," Hawkins replied.

"With no law," Lomax said, "you should have a private security force."

"You mean gunmen?" Westin asked. "I also said I wasn't going to be that kind of mayor."

"Somebody's gotta get that money back here," Lomax said. "You think that lady sheriff's gonna do it?"

"I think right now," Mayor Westin said, "she's all we've got."

***

Sheriff Holliday walked into the Town Council meeting room and felt all eyes on her.

"What's going on?" she asked. "Why was I summoned here?"

"Because you're our sheriff," the Mayor said.

"Since when?"

"Since we need one," Lomax said.

"Have a seat," Mayor Westin said. "Please. Let me tell you why you're here."

She sat and listened.

"How much?" she asked, when the mayor was finished. "How much was taken?"

"Upward of fifty thousand dollars," Westin said.

"*That* much!?" Williams said, in surprise.

"I'm afraid so."

"Do you have any idea who might've taken it?" Holliday asked.

"No," Westin said, "but it was somebody who knew how to crack a safe."

"We need to get that money back," Hawkins said. "The town is broke without it."

"Can you do it?" the Mayor asked.

"Of course I can," she said. "You people are the only one's with doubts."

"If you bring that money back," Lomax said, "and the thieves, the whole town will accept you as their sheriff."

"Then consider it done," she said. She looked at Mayor Westin. "I need to see where it was taken from."

"Of course," he said. "Follow me."

The mayor led the sheriff out of the room and up to his office, leaving the Town Council members alone.

"We made a mistake," Hawkins said, "backing him."

"Yeah, we did," Lomax asked.

"So what do we do?" Williams asked.

"As soon as that money is back in the safe," Hawkins said, "we get ourselves a new mayor."

"And the sheriff?" Lomax asked.

"She'll have to go, too."

Chapter Nine

Sheriff Holliday examined the safe, then turned to look at the mayor.

"It wasn't broken into," she said. "It was opened. As if someone knew the combination."

"Except I'm the only one who knows it," he said, "and I didn't open it."

"Who in town knows how to open a safe without dynamite?" she asked.

"I'd say nobody."

"Somebody must," she said, "otherwise . . ."

"Otherwise what?"

"There's a stranger in town who did this," she offered.

"How many strangers are in town?" he asked.

She put her hands on her hips.

"Just one."

***

Holliday went back to her office to think. The town fathers were actually depending on her, but she didn't know the first thing about getting the money back. She sat down at her desk and set her hat aside.

She was still sitting there an hour later when a man named Tige Bellamy came in.

"Sheriff," he said.

Usually, Bellamy looked pretty drunk, but it was early in the day and he was still fairly lucid.

"Bellamy," she said. "What brings you here?"

"I thought you should know," he said, "I saw the Gunsmith near City Hall."

"When?"

"Early this mornin'."

"This is important, Bellamy," she said, leaning forward. "Did you see him coming out, or going in?"

Bellamy gave that some thought.

"Uh, comin' out—no! Goin' in. No, wait—"

"Was he carrying anything?"

"N-no—wait, yeah, he was."

"What?"

"Uh, a bag . . . of some kind."

"Uh-huh." She took a coin from her vest pocket and tossed it to him. He caught it.

"T-thanks, Sheriff." He pocketed the coin and left.

She put on her hat and left the office, to go and find the Gunsmith.

***

Since Clint's hotel dining room only served break-fast, he decided to give it a try. He was halfway through a plate of ham-and-eggs that was just palatable when the sheriff appeared at the doorway. There were several other diners who watched her walk across the room to him.

"I thought I was the only stranger in town," he said, looking around.

"You are," she said. "These folks live in the hotel. Mind if I sit?"

"Of course not," he said. "I wouldn't recommend the breakfast, but the coffee's all right." He'd found that out when he'd had coffee there with her the day before.

"I actually haven't had breakfast yet," she said, waving at the waiter, "so I'll chance it."

The waiter came hurrying over.

"Yes, ma'am."

"I'll have what he's having," she said.

"Comin' up."

The waiter turned and hurried to the kitchen.

"What did I do to deserve this visit?" he asked.

"Nothing, really," she said. "Can you open a safe?"

"What?"

"It's just a question," she said. "Can you open a safe?"

"With a combination, sure."

"But not without?"

"Are you asking me if I'm a safecracker?" he asked. "The answer's no, that's not one of my talents."

"Were you anywhere near City Hall this morning?"

"No," he said. "I woke up and came down here."

"That's what I thought."

The waiter came with her breakfast. They waited for him to leave before speaking again.

"What's going on?" he asked.

"The safe in the mayor's office was robbed last night," she said. "All of the town's money was taken. A witness told me this morning that he saw you near City Hall."

"That was a lie."

"I thought so," she said, "and now I know so."

"How are you involved?" he asked.

"The mayor and the Town Council asked me to find the money."

"Well," he said, "I guess they're taking you more seriously."

"They don't have a choice," she said. "There's no one else."

Chapter Ten

"What I need to do," she said, after breakfast, "is question that witness again."

"Would you like me to come along?" he asked.

"It might put a good scare into him if you did," she admitted. "He's sort of the town drunk, but I still don't think he's afraid of me. And he was real confused about what he saw, and when he saw it."

"Then maybe together," Clint offered, "we can get him thinking straight."

"That sounds good to me," she said.

Clint paid for breakfast and they left the hotel.

***

"His name's Bellamy, and he's going to be at one of the saloons."

"This early?" Clint asked. "Are you sure?"

"I tossed him a coin," she said. "It'll be burning a hole in his pocket."

They checked the Moon Shadow Saloon first and found Bellamy there, bellied up to the bar with a beer in front of him.

"'mornin', Sheriff," the bartender greeted. There were no other customers, but he moved down to the opposite end of the bar, anyway.

Bellamy froze, then turned his head to look at Sheriff Holliday."

"Hello, Bellamy," she said.

"S-sheriff," he said, nervously.

"I brought somebody here to meet you," she said. "This is Clint Adams, the Gunsmith."

Bellamy looked at Clint with wide, frightened eyes.

"Does he look familiar?" the sheriff asked.

"Huh?"

"Is this the man you saw in front of City Hall early this morning?"

"Um . . ." Bellamy said, staring at Clint.

"Do you want me to come closer?" Clint asked.

"Huh? Oh, no, nonono," Bellamy said, "you don't gotta come closer." He looked at the Sheriff. "No, this ain't the man."

"So then you didn't see the Gunsmith in front of City Hall?" she repeated.

"No, Ma'am, I didn't." He looked down at the beer he'd bought with the coin she'd tossed him, then quickly drank it down before she could take it away from him.

"Now Bellamy," she said, "we need to know who told you to say you saw the Gunsmith this morning."

"Huh? N-nobody tol' me," Bellamy said. "I just made a mistake."

"Yeah, you did," Clint commented, "when you said my name." This time he did step closer. "Now you're going to tell us who told you to do that, aren't you?"

Bellamy cringed and said, "Yessir!"

***

"Where do we find Sam Tennant?" Clint asked Holliday as they stepped outside. "I assume you know since you didn't ask Bellamy."

"I know," she said. "He works out at the Big Fork spread."

"Big Fork," Clint said. "Would that be Lawrence Crandall's place?"

"That's it."

"Then he might be one of the three men I talked to last night in the Moon Shadow."

"Ah," she said, "he was with Collins."

Clint nodded.

"Him and a man named Pete."

"That probably puts Collins squarely behind this," she said. "One of them is probably the safe man."

"I guess you'll be heading out there," Clint said.

"I don't expect to find them there," she said, "but I can talk to Mr. Crandall and see what he knows."

"You think Crandall might be behind it?" he asked.

"As far as I know he's an honest man," she replied.

"But the mayor's been cutting his spread into little pieces, hasn't he?" Clint asked.

"He has."

"Don't you think that might be pushing an honest man a little too far?"

"That could be," she said. "I'll know more after I talk to him."

"Want company?"

"I'd say not for this," she said, "it's just going to be a conversation, but who knows what's out there? So, yes, I'd appreciate it."

"Okay," Clint said, "I've got plenty of time. After all, I'm not leaving town until tomorrow . . . right?"

"Right," she said.

He watched her walk off in the direction of the livery stable, supposedly to get her horse. He followed.

Chapter Eleven

The Crandall ranch looked to have seen better days. The barn needed a paint job, and the house needed some work on the roof and the siding. The corral had some broken sections, which was probably why there were no horses inside.

"This looks like it might have been a nice place, at one time," Clint said, as they approached the house.

"Biggest in the county," Sheriff Holliday said. "Until Mayor Westin went to work."

"Why did he have it in for Mr. Crandall?" Clint asked.

"Nobody knows," she said. "It's just one of the things he started doing as soon as he got elected. A lot of folks think a bank or a stageline should've come first. If it had, then maybe all that money wouldn't have been in his office safe."

"What do you think the chances are that he took it himself?" Clint asked.

"I considered it," she said, "but that's not the impression I got this morning. He seems really rattled by what's happened."

"Then why didn't he take steps to make sure it didn't happen?" Clint asked. "Like armed guards on City Hall?"

"He apparently thought that would send the wrong kind of message to the people in town."

They reined in their horses in front of the house and dismounted. Clint looked around.

"Where're the hands?" he wondered.

"Most of them left," she said. "The rest are . . . I don't know."

"What about Collins and his friends?"

"Normally, they'd be around here," she said.

They mounted the steps and knocked on the door. After a few moments it was opened by a white-haired woman.

"We're here to see Mr. Crandall," Holliday said.

The woman nodded and said, "Please, come in."

They entered, closing the door behind them. Clint looked at the large entry hall, then noticed all the dust. The place needed a good cleaning.

"Wait here," the woman said, and walked off slowly.

"His wife?" he asked.

"Housekeeper," Holliday said. "His wife died a lot of years ago."

They waited and just when Clint started to think she wasn't coming back, she shuffled back into view and waved at them.

"This way."

They followed her to another room where a white-haired, bone-thin man sat in a large armchair with his head bowed.

"Mr. Crandall," Sheriff Holliday said.

"Sheriff." He looked at the woman. "That'll be all, Belinda."

The old woman nodded and withdrew.

"What can I do for you, Sheriff?"

"Mr. Crandall, this is Clint Adams."

"The famous Gunsmith," the older man said. "What brings you both here?"

"We're looking for your men," she said. "Collins, Pete and Sam."

"Selby and Tennant," the older man said. "Why do you need them?"

"The town's been robbed," she said. "All the cash was taken from the mayor's safe. We think they did it."

"What makes you think that?"

"Because they tried to pin it on me," Clint said. "They had a phony witness say he saw me near City Hall this morning. It wasn't me."

"What about the mayor?" he asked. "He could've done it himself."

"I'm still considering that possibility," she admitted. "But I need to talk to those three men."

Crandall didn't answer. He remained silent long enough for Clint to wonder if something had happened. His skin was like parchment paper, and his eyes were cloudy. If they hadn't still been open, Clint might've thought he was dead. But then he spoke.

"So you're finally acting like a real sheriff?" he asked Holliday.

"Yes, I am," she said. "Somebody has to."

"Collins and his men left," he said. "They were the last ones."

"When did they go?" she asked.

"This morning."

"Do you know if one of them had the ability to open a safe?" Clint asked.

"That'd probably be Sam Tennant," Crandall said. "I forgot the combination to my safe one day. He got it open, just using his fingers and his ear."

Holliday looked at Clint.

"It was them." She looked at Crandall. "Did you send them to town to steal the money?"

"And why would I do that?" he asked. "My ranch may have shrunk, but I have my own money."

"To get back at the mayor?"

"I want to get back at him," Crandall said, "but not the whole town. So no, it wasn't me."

"Is Collins smart enough to have planned this?" she asked.

"No," Crandall said, "you should look for somebody else, somebody older who he'd listen to."

"Any ideas who that might be?" Holliday asked.

Crandall hesitated, then said, "I have one."

Chapter Twelve

They rode back to town and stopped in front of the Moon Shadow. When they went inside Clint saw a different bartender working.

"Where's Benny?" he asked.

"He had to go do somethin'," the young bartender said. "Asked me to watch the place."

"For how long?" Sheriff Holliday asked.

"I dunno."

"When did he leave?" Clint asked.

"About an hour ago."

Clint looked at Holliday.

"He can't have gone far," Clint said. "He's the only one who'll have any idea where Collins and the others went."

"I thought I was going to have to track them," she said. "I guess I'll have to catch him, first."

"Do you want me to come with you?"

"It's the town's money," she said. "I'll get a posse together."

"Let me know how that goes," he said.

***

It didn't go.

Everywhere she went to ask about a posse, somebody had an excuse.

"I got a business to run," one man said.

"My wife won't let me go," another said.

"I ain't a lawman," more than one said.

And the response she got from most of the men she talked to was, "You're kiddin', right . . . *Sheriff*?"

She found Clint having a drink at the Hanging man Saloon.

"How did it go?" he asked.

"Not well," she said, "and I can't spend any more time begging the men in this town to ride with me."

"Let's get some supplies and leave in half-an-hour, then," he told her.

"You're coming with me?"

"Do you know how to track and read sign?" he asked.

"Not a clue."

"Then yes," he said, "I'm going with you."

***

Holliday stopped at the mayor's office to fill him in.

"I'm sorry, Sheriff," he said, "but it doesn't surprise me. The men in this town just aren't the law enforcement type. That's why you're wearing the badge. I mean, I'd go with you myself, but I'm a politician—"

"I get it, Mr. Mayor," she said, cutting him off.

"You're sure it wasn't the Gunsmith?" he asked, then.

"He didn't have any reason to do it," she said.

"Fifty thousand dollars isn't reason enough?"

"How would he have known about it?" she asked. "No, it wasn't him, but he's going to help me find the ones who did do it."

"You know who they are?"

"I believe," she said, "it was three men who were working for Lawrence Crandall."

"Crandall!" Westin hissed. "Is he behind this?"

"No, they were just working for him, but they left this morning." She didn't explain that Benny might be involved. "We'll be leaving right away. I just wanted to let you know."

"If you get this done, Sheriff," he said, "the entire town will be in your debt."

"Don't worry, Mr. Mayor," she said. "I'll bring the money back."

She left City Hall and found Clint waiting out front with the horses, and supplies in two gunny sacks, one hanging from each saddle.

"You ready?" he asked.

"Ready."

***

Benny the bartender had gotten his horse from the livery. The hostler pointed out the stall it had been in.

"Take a good look at these tracks," Clint told Holliday. "That's what we're going to be looking for."

She pointed.

"Either his horse's hoof has a chip in it, or the shoe does."

"Whichever it is," Clint said, "that's what we're going to track."

They left the livery and mounted up.

"I hope he takes us to Collins and the others," she said, "and not just another town where he's got a woman."

"That's what we're going to find out," he told her.

The tracks came out of the livery and went back toward the main street. On the street there were too many tracks from horses, wagons and boots to pick one set out. But they continued on through town and out. After about a mile more, there they were.

"There," Clint said, pointing.

"I see them!" Holliday said, excitedly.

They started to follow the tracks.

***

Collins, Sam and Pete were three hours on the trail from the Big Fork when Collins reined them in just to give the horses a breather.

Pete asked, "Where are we headed?"

"Benny told us to meet him in a town called Medicine Bow," Collins said.

"We have all the money," Sam said, "so why are we meetin' him?"

"Because without him we'd have nothin'," Collins said. "I keep my word, Sam. We said it would be a four-way split, and it will be."

"How much further is it gonna be?" Pete asked. "I'm gettin' hungry."

"Have some beef jerky," Collins said. "We're still a few hours away."

Pete and Sam exchanged a glance as Collins started to move again.

Chapter Thirteen

Benny Gordon knew that biding his time in the town of "Pleasant" would eventually pay off. He owned the Moon Shadow Saloon, but knew it was worth next to nothing, because now that the town had been robbed, it would dry up for sure.

All he needed to get the job done were the right men, and tending bar enabled him to feel out the likely candidates. When he met Collins, Selby and Tennant, he knew he had them. Now he just had to hope they wouldn't try to cut him out. He thought he could depend on Collins, but Pete Selby and Sam Tennant were another matter. He was going to have to depend on Collins to keep them in line. But if he got to Medicine Bow and didn't find the three men there, he had the option of going back to Pleasant and finding somebody who might want to buy a saloon.

***

Clint did not consider himself an expert tracker, but along the way he taught Sheriff Holliday whatever he knew.

"Some of this sounds so simple," she commented.

"There's so much more I don't know," he told her. "But we have enough to follow Benny."

"If it's Benny," Holliday said.

"It has to be," Clint said. "We've been following the same tracks for hours. It's him."

"Then where's he going?"

"Somewhere to meet with the others," Clint said. "Do you have any idea what towns lie ahead of us?"

"A lot," she said. "If Benny doesn't lead us right to one, we'll have to try them all."

"Then let's hope he does," Clint said.

***

Medicine Bow had everything Collins, Sam and Pete needed to pass the time waiting for Benny.

Pete spent the time playing poker in one of the saloons.

Sam spent his time drinking.

Collins spent his in the whorehouse on the edge of town . . .

The naked blonde rolled over in bed, onto her belly, cradled her chin in her hands and looked at Collins.

"You've been in town two days, and you've spent them all with me," she said. "Do you love me?"

"Hell, no," he said. "I'm payin' you."

"Good," she said, "'cause I don't love you, either."

"Of course you don't," he said. "You're a whore."

"And you're a bastard!" she snapped.

"Good," he said, "we understand each other."

He grabbed her and flipped her onto her back. She was thin, almost scrawny, with small breasts that had very large nipples and aureole. He found them mesmerizing. The same with the heavy matt of blonde hair between her legs. He liked to probe through it until he found her wetness, first with his fingers, and then with his cock.

He drove himself into her and she gasped, her eyes going wide. The look on her face was one of pure lust.

"That's it," she said, imploring him, "come on, harder!"

He had fucked many women, but this one was the first he'd encountered who liked it hard. Most women found him too rough, sometimes causing him to knock them around so he could do what he wanted. But this one, this Laura, she was right there with him—hard, and fast.

"Yeah," she gasped, as he fucked her, "oh yeah, baby, that's it . . ."

He grabbed her ankles and spread her wide, continued to pound away at her until her eyes bulged and she screamed . . .

***

"Does anybody ever come runnin' up here when you scream like that?" he asked.

"They did," she said, "in the beginnin', but not anymore. They know how I like it, and when I get it, I scream. But I ain't had it like this for a long time, Collins. You ain't plannin' on leavin' anytime soon, are ya?"

"I'm waitin' for a man," he said. "When he gets here, we'll have to see."

"Well then," she said, reaching for him, "I hope he don't get here for a long time."

***

They tracked Benny to a town called Perryville. When they checked in with the local sheriff he said, "I got somethin' to show you."

He took them to the undertaker's and showed them a body lying on a table.

"Do you know 'im?" Sheriff Al Tate asked. He was a big, florid-faced man in his fifties who seemed willing to accept the lady sheriff.

Clint and Holliday both recognized the man.

"That's Benny," she said, "the man we've been tracking."

"What happened?" Clint asked.

"He got to town, stopped in the saloon for a beer, got into a fight and got killed. Simple as that."

"Where's the man who killed him?" Clint asked.

"Dead," Tate said. "I had to kill him."

They all left the undertaker's and went back to the lawman's office.

After that Clint and Holliday stopped in a café for a hot meal and to discuss their next move.

"Now what?" she asked.

"Like you said," Clint replied, "we'll have to start checking towns one-by-one."

"That'll take forever."

"We're looking for fifty thousand dollars," he reminded her. "I think that's worth the time."

"What makes you think we'll find them in a town?" she asked. "They could be moving on."

"I think we've got a few days," he said, "if they're waiting for Benny to split the money."

"What if they double-crossed him, and never intended to wait, at all?"

"Then we'll have to go back to Pleasant without it," he said. "And you'll probably be out of a job."

Chapter Fourteen

In two days, they checked four towns, and didn't find any sign of the three men.

When they rode into Medicine Bow, it was their fifth in three days.

"My horse needs some rest," Holliday said.

"We'll check around, talk to the local law, and spend the night," he said.

"And maybe in the morning we should head back, Clint," she said.

"You've had it?" he asked.

"How long can we do this?" she asked.

"That's up to you," he said. "I can't tell you what to do, Sheriff. I mean, I can tell you how to track, but I can't tell you how long to do your job."

"My job," she said, shaking her head.

They stopped at a hotel and got two rooms, then Clint took the horses to the livery. He met her in the lobby, and they headed for the marshal's office.

***

"A woman sheriff," the local marshal said. "Well, don't that beat all."

Marshal Ben Denby was in his forties and seemed to have the attitude of a much older man, very set in his ways.

"Don't that beat *all*," he said, again.

"Marshal," she said, "we're looking for three men."

"And the Gunsmith," Marshal Denby went on. "Don't that beat—"

"Marshal," Clint said, "we don't have time—"

"Three men, you say?" the marshal asked. "What'd they do?"

"They robbed my town," she said. "Took fifty thousand dollars."

The marshal's eyes widened.

"Don't that beat—they robbed the bank?"

"We don't really have a bank yet," Holliday said, "but they robbed a safe, yes."

"Why do you think they'd be here?"

"They're supposed to be meeting up with a fourth man, probably to split the money," Clint said. "We'd been going from town-to-town."

"I thought you said you was trackin' them?"

"We were tracking the fourth man," she said. "We found him, dead."

"So we're going town-to-town," Clint said. "This is our fifth in three days."

"Have you had any strangers here?" she asked.

"Nope," the marshal lied, "not a one."

Chapter Fifteen

After Clint Adams and Sheriff Holliday left his office, Marshal Denby used the back door and headed for the whorehouse.

"Marshal," Lulu, the madam, said at the door. "What brings you here? Your wife finally kick you out?"

"I'm not here for a poke, Lulu," Denby told the middle-aged madam. "I'm here to talk to one of your johns."

"Which one?"

"The stranger."

"Collins? He's upstairs, with Laura. You want me to go up and get 'im?"

"No," the lawman said, "I'll go up. I'm just gonna talk to him."

"No shooting, Denby," she said. "I'll charge the town for any damage you do. Got it?"

"I got it."

"Room five."

Denby went up the stairs, down the hall to Laura's room and knocked. A skinny, naked blonde answered the door.

"Marshal?" she said.

"I need to talk to Collins," he said.

She turned and looked at Collins, who was on the bed.

"The law wants to talk to you?" she said.

Collins rolled over and made a grab for his gun.

"You won't need that," Denby said. "At least, not for me."

Collins stopped.

"Take a walk, Laura," Denby said.

She turned and looked at Collins.

"Go ahead," he said. "It's okay." He tossed her a robe, which she pulled on and then stepped into the hall. Denby entered the room and closed the door.

"What's on your mind, Marshal?" Collins asked.

"Fifty thousand dollars," Denby said.

Collins reclined on the bed and put his hands behind his head.

"I'm listenin'."

***

"What do you think?" Clint asked, as they walked away from the marshal's office.

"About what?" Sheriff Holliday asked.

"The marshal," Clint said. "Was he telling the truth?"

"Why wouldn't he?"

"Because all lawmen aren't honest, Sheriff," he said.

"You didn't think that in the other towns," she pointed out.

"I've got a bad feeling about this Marshal Denby," Clint said. "I don't think he's the old bumpkin he wants us to think he is."

"So what do you want to do?"

"Let's talk to some bartenders and see if the marshal was lying."

***

"Did they kill 'im?" Collins asked.

"No," Denby said, "according to them they found him dead."

"That sure as hell would explain why he's not here," Collins said. "And what's your interest, marshal? Why the warnin'?"

"I want his share," Denby said.

"A fourth?" Collins said. "That's enough for you?"

"I ain't greedy."

"And what do we get for that?"

"Hey, I warned you," Denby said, "and I'll keep them off your trail."

Collins took only a few seconds to consider his options. He'd been willing to pay Benny his fourth, so what was the difference now that the bartender was dead?

"Okay, you got a deal."

"Don't you have to check with your partners?"

Collins got off the bed and pulled on his trousers.

"They'll go along."

"Adams and a lady sheriff are in town, so you'll have to avoid them," Marshal Denby said. "You should pay me and get out of town as soon as possible."

Collins knew he had to get to Selby and Tennant quick, before Adams and that lady sheriff from Pleasant stumbled across them.

"Where are you gonna be so I can pay ya?" he asked, strapping on his gun.

"My office," Denby said. "Come to the back door and bang on it. I'll hear ya."

The two men left the room and went downstairs, where Collins handed Lulu some money.

"Laura's sure gonna be sorry to see you go, honey," Lulu said.

"I know," Collins said. "Tell her I said I'm sorry, but I hadda go."

"Come back soon," she called to him, as the two men went out the front door.

Chapter Sixteen

Sam Tennant was playing poker and Pete Selby was drinking in the Ten Gallon Saloon when Collins got there. Thankfully, the Gunsmith and the sheriff were nowhere in sight.

"Let's go," he said to Pete, who was standing at the bar.

"Where?" Selby asked.

"You want your share?"

Selby slammed down his empty mug.

"Let's go!" he said.

"Get Sam and meet me in the back room."

"Right."

Collins pointed at the back room and the bartender nodded.

Selby went to the poker table and nudged Sam Tennant.

"Let's go."

"Where?" Tennant asked.

"Collins wants us in the back room."

"Wait til I finish this hand."

Selby leaned down and said, "Is there fifty thousand in that pot?"

Tennant dropped his cards to the table and said, "I'm out!" He stood and followed Selby to the back.

As the three men sat down at the round table in the room, the bartender brought in three beers.

"Thanks, Jackson," Collins said.

"Benny on the way?" Jackson asked.

"I'll tell ya later," Collins said.

Jackson nodded and left.

"What's goin' on?" Sam Tennant asked.

"Benny's dead?"

"What?" Pete Selby snapped.

"How?" Tennant asked.

"He was on his way here when he stopped in a saloon in some town and got himself killed," Collins explained.

"So," Tennant said, "a three-way split."

"Not exactly," Collins said, and explained.

"So they're in town right now?" Selby asked. "Lookin' for us?"

"Looks that way."

"We gotta get out," Tennant said.

"And we will, as soon as we pay the marshal Benny's share," Collins said.

"Look," Selby said, "give us our shares and then you go pay the marshal."

"No," Collins said, "we started this together and we'll finish it together."

"And how do you think Jackson's gonna react?" Selby asked. "Benny was his friend."

"I'll explain it to him."

"How?" Tennant asked.

"I'll tell him that the Gunsmith and that Lady sheriff killed him."

"He'll go after them," Selby said.

"Exactly."

"I get it," Tennant said. "We'll leave town in the confusion."

"Exactly."

"But are we really gonna pay the marshal Benny's share?" Selby asked.

Collins smiled.

"Let's just say we're gonna pay the marshal a visit before we leave."

***

Collins instructed Selby and Tennant to stay out of sight while he went and talked to Jackson at the bar.

"What's goin' on?" the bartender asked when Collins appeared.

"I've got some bad news for you, Jackson." He looked around, made sure no one was standing within earshot. Most of the patrons there were seated at tables.

"What is it?"

"Benny's not comin'."

"Why not?"

"He's dead."

"What?" The big bartender glared at Collins. "How?"

"He was tracked and killed by the sheriff from Pleasant and Clint Adams."

"That lady sheriff?"

"That's right," Collins said, "and they're here. Me and my men have to get outta here, Jackson."

"You go ahead," Jackson said. "I'll have them taken care of."

"So you don't want Benny's share of the money?" Collins asked.

"No," Jackson said, "I don't need money. That was Benny's thing."

"Then why go after them?" Collins asked. "Because he was your friend?"

"No," Jackson said, "not because he was my friend. Benny was my brother."

Chapter Seventeen

Jackson knew that Clint Adams and the lady sheriff were looking for Collins and his men. That meant they'd be checking saloons. All he had to do was wait.

***

Clint and Holliday checked the Ten Gallon Saloon second. As they entered, Clint put his hand on Holliday's arm.

"What is it?" she asked.

"This doesn't feel right," he said. "Be ready."

"Right."

They looked around, saw several of the tables occupied, but there was no one at the bar, save the bartender, a big man in his forties.

"Welcome," he said. "What can I getcha?"

"Some information," Sheriff Holliday said. "We're looking for three men."

"Is that right?" the bartender asked. "Look around. There's more than three here."

Clint looked around, saw the eight men in the room staring at them.

"Do you know them?" Holliday asked. "Collins, Selby and Tennant?"

"I knew Benny," the bartender said.

"What?" Holliday asked. "How?"

"He was my brother," the big bartender said, "and you killed him."

"Who told you that?" Clint asked. "Collins?"

"Which one of you did it?" the man asked. "Probably you, right? You're the Gunsmith."

"I'm the Gunsmith," Clint said, "but I didn't kill your brother, and neither did Sheriff Holliday."

"Then who did?"

"Some man in some saloon in some town," Clint said. "And then the lawman in that town killed him. So you see, your brother's death has been avenged. We're looking for the three men he was working with."

"You were tracking him," the bartender said. "You got him killed."

Clint could see the man was intent on his vengeance. And it was going to be messy.

"Get ready," he said to Holliday.

"Damn," she said.

The bartender yelled, "Now!"

***

Collins banged on the rear door of the jail just as they heard the shots.

"About time," the marshal said, when he opened it. "Sounds like it's started."

Collins didn't answer.

Marshal Denby looked at all three of them. None seemed to be carrying anything.

"Where's my money?" he asked.

Again, Collins didn't answer, but this time he simply drew his gun and fired one round into the marshal's belly. The man staggered back and fell. Collins stepped in and looked down at him.

"Consider this your payment," he said.

He turned holstered his gun and said, "Let's get the hell out of here."

***

Clint pushed the lady sheriff to one side and yelled, "Take cover!"

He drew and fired a round into the bartender's chest as the eight men all stood up and started firing. As lead flew all around him, he leaped over the bar. At the same time, Sheriff Holliday upended a table and took cover behind it.

At that point, many more tables hit the floor, and the shooting stopped.

"Okay," Clint called out, "this bartender's dead, like his brother. What are we fighting about, now? Think about it."

Clint could see Sheriff Holliday from where he was, so he motioned for her to be patient. She nodded but kept her gun in hand.

"You men don't even have to drop your guns," Clint said. "Just stand up and walk out. It's all over."

Nothing happened, and then one-by-one the men stood from behind the overturned tables and walked out the batwing doors. Some of them had their shoulders hunched, as if waiting to be shot, but eventually Clint and Sheriff Holliday were alone in the saloon.

Holliday stood up from behind her table and Clint came around from behind the bar, where the dead bartender was lying on the floor.

"How did you know that'd work?" she asked.

"I didn't," he said. "I just hoped they'd realize with Benny's brother dead, they would be fighting—and dying—for nothing."

"Luck, then," Holliday said. "Now what?"

"Now let's go talk to the marshal," Clint said. "He must have some idea where Collins and the others were going."

Together, they left the saloon.

***

They entered the marshal's office and found it empty.

"Let's check the cell block," Clint said.

That's where they found Marshal Denby, on the floor, bleeding from a belly wound.

"What took you so long?" he asked, blood trickling from his mouth.

Clint and Holliday knelt by him and examined his wound.

"Ya can't do nothin'," Denby said. "I only got a few minutes more."

"Who shot you?" Clint asked.

"Collins."

"Were the others with him?"

"Yeah."

"Do you know where they were going?" Holliday asked.

"N-no." His eyes fluttered. "T-they double-crossed me."

"You were claiming Benny's cut," Clint said. "You told them we were here."

Denby could only nod, then a great spurt of blood came from his mouth, and he died.

Holliday looked at Clint.

"Now what?"

"That's up to you," he said, "Sheriff."

Chapter Eighteen

They went to the undertaker first, to get the marshal's body taken care of, and then to the livery stable to talk to the hostler.

"Sure thing, Sheriff," the old man said. "Three fellers rode out a little while ago."

"Do you know what direction they went?" Clint asked.

"Nossir," he said. "I don't. They rode out my front door and was gone."

"All right," the sheriff said, "thanks." She looked at Clint. "Buy you a drink?"

**

At the Ten Gallon Saloon they stood at the bar and ordered beer. The place was empty but for a few men seated at tables, even though it was late in the day. And it didn't seem they had any trouble replacing their bartender.

"Two beers," the barman said, setting them down. He was a tall man in his forties, who looked uncomfortable behind the bar.

"Are you the owner?" Clint asked.

"Nope. The owner got killed earlier today," the man said. "But you know that. You killed 'im."

"And you're still open?"

The man shrugged.

"What else are we gonna do?" he asked. "Some of us decided to take turns behind the bar and keep the place open until somebody says otherwise."

The man walked away and began cleaning glasses.

"What do you want to do now, Sheriff?" Clint asked, turning his attention to Holliday.

"Why," she asked, "have you never asked me my first name?"

"You're the sheriff," he said. "That's what matters."

"I'm a town sheriff," she said. "I'm already out of my jurisdiction. I've got no authority, here."

"Still," Clint said, "you're wearing a badge, and the town law here has been killed."

"That's not my business," she said. "Only that money and the three men who stole it was my business. And now they're on the run, again. The way I see it, I've got three options."

"Chase them," Clint said, "track them, or . . . what?"

"Or go back home," she said.

"You mean give up?"

"How much longer should I try?" she asked. "How much longer will you stay with it? This isn't your job, at all."

"That's true," he said. "It's not."

"But whether you stay with me or not, how much more time could I give it, and how far should I go?"

"Those aren't questions I can answer," he said. "I've known lawmen to chase outlaws to Mexico and Canada, where they had no authority. And I've known them to go as far as the county line and turn back."

She sipped her beer.

"I think I'll stay the night in the hotel," she said, "and head back tomorrow."

"How long do you think you'll hold onto your job if you go back empty handed?" he asked.

"I don't know," she said. "I guess I'll have to figure out if I even want to keep the job."

"And if you don't?" he asked. "What will you do then?"

She shrugged.

"I don't really know," she said.

"Could you go back to teaching?"

"Maybe," she said. "I'd have to find a town that needs a teacher, but . . . I don't know."

They stood there and sipped their beers for a while before one of them spoke again.

"Delores," she said.

"Huh?"

"That's my first name," she said. "Delores."

Chapter Nineteen

Clint and Sheriff Delores Holliday went to the hotel and each got a room. He was deep into a Mark Twain story when there was a knock on his door. He had the book under his arm and the gun in his hand when he answered it.

"You mind if I come in?" Delores Holliday asked.

"Come on in," he said, backing away from the door. She entered and he closed it.

"I'm still struggling, trying to decide what to do," she said. Clint put his gun in the holster that was hanging from the bed post.

"Sit," he said, "let's talk about it."

"I thought it might be better to get my mind off everything for a while," she said, sitting on the bed.

"I could loan you my Twain book—" he started.

"No," she said, "I had another idea."

She stood up, unstrapped her gunbelt, walked around and hung it from the other bedpost. That done, she started to unbutton her shirt.

"Delores—" he said, but he stopped talking when she peeled off the shirt, revealing herself to be naked beneath it. Her full breasts bobbed into view, striking him dumb. The nipples were dark pink, and distended.

"If you're not interested," she said, "I can stop here and go."

"No," he said, "I'm interested—very interested."

She smiled, sat at the foot of the bed and pulled off her boots, the movements causing her breasts to jiggle enticingly. That done, she stood and slid her trousers down, letting them drop to her ankles where she stepped from them and kicked them to a corner.

"I'm not a young girl anymore," she said, "but I think I'm holding up pretty well."

"No argument from me" he said.

"Well then," she went on, "what are you waiting for?"

He kept his eyes on her while he sat and removed his boots. She did not seem shy about her nudity and watched with interest while he undressed. Soon he was as naked as she, his cock already at more than half mast.

"Well," she said, looking down at his crotch, "that'll keep more than my mind busy."

She walked to him and took his cock in her hands, began to stroke it gently while tilting her head up and kissing him. He kissed her back, sliding his hands down her naked back to cup her buttocks and pull her closer.

The heat of their bodies meeting increased the temperature in the room. By the time they tumbled to the bed together, they were both sweating . . .

***

The bartender looked up from his dirty glass as someone came through the batwing doors and entered the Ten Gallon Saloon.

"Hello, Mr. Mars," he said.

"What happened in here today, Lew?" Tom Mars asked. Medicine Bow didn't have a mayor, but Tom Mars was the head of the Town Council. It wasn't much of a town, but folks looked to the fifty-five year old business man to run things.

"Jackson finally bit off more than he could chew," Lew said. "He tried to take on the Gunsmith."

"What the hell is the Gunsmith doing in town?" Mars asked.

"I only know what Jackson said," Lew answered. "Had somethin' to do with his brother Benny gettin' killed."

"That one was always a troublemaker," Mars said. "Do you know that the marshal was killed?"

"I heard."

"Have you heard anything about who did it?"

"No," Lew said. "I only heard that the Gunsmith killed Jackson."

"Didn't the idiot have any backup?"

"Eight men."

"What happened to them?"

"After Jackson was killed, they all left."

"Were you one of the eight, Lew?"

"No, sir."

"You talk to any of them?"

"Two," Lew said. "Seems none of them wanted to go up against Clint Adams."

"And did Adams have help?"

"Somebody said somethin' about a lady sheriff."

Mars scowled.

"Give me a whiskey."

Lew poured him a shot, which he tossed off.

"Jackson's no loss," he said, "but now we don't have a lawman."

"I heard Adams was tracking down some men," Lew said. "Maybe they're the ones who killed Marshal Denby."

"Yes, maybe they are," Mars said. "Do you know where Adams is now?"

"I heard he took a hotel room."

"You hear a lot of things, Lew," Mars said.

"I keep my ears open."

"You going to keep this place open?"

"Me and some of the boys is gonna take turns," Lew said. "I guess we'll do that until somebody closes us down."

"Let's worry about one thing at a time," Mars said, and left the saloon.

Chapter Twenty

Clint found Delores Holliday's body of great interest to him. He got her onto her back and explored her with his hands and mouth until she was grabbing at him, trying to pull him up on top of her.

"Come on, come on," she said, "you're driving me crazy."

He slid atop her, and then into her wetness with ease. He nuzzled her breasts while he pumped in and out and her body was wracked by waves of pleasure just as somebody knocked on the door.

"Oh Jesus," she whispered into his ear, "who the hell is that?"

"We could ignore it," he offered.

Somebody then pounded on the door.

"I'll see who it is," he said.

"Send them away!" she kissed.

He pulled on his trousers, palmed his gun and went to the door.

"Who is it?"

"Mr. Adams? My name is Tom Mars. I'm the head of the Town Council here in Medicine Bow. Can we talk?"

"About what?"

"Well," Mars said, "two men have been killed since you arrived. I'd, uh, like to discuss that."

Clint hesitated a moment, the said, "Wait downstairs in the lobby."

"What the hell—" Delores gasped.

"I'll go down and talk to him," he said.

She pointed at the bulge in his pants and said, "Maybe I should take care of that first."

"Well," he said, "all right, but make it quick."

She pulled his trousers down to his ankles, then got to her knees and took his hard cock into her mouth. She had no intention of making it quick . . .

***

Tom Mars was starting to get impatient when Clint Adams came down the stairs.

"I thought you were going to leave me waiting," he said.

"Believe me, the thought crossed my mind," Clint said. "We've done a lot of riding and we're looking to get some sleep."

"We?"

"I'm here with Sheriff Holliday from the town of Pleasant."

"Can we go someplace, have a drink and talk?" Mars asked.

"No, I think right here's fine. What's on your mind?"

"We have a dead businessman and marshal," Mars said. "We'd like to know what happened."

"Your dead businessman tried to bushwhack us," Clint said. "We took care of it with only one fatality."

"What about the marshal?"

"We tracked three men here," Clint said. "We're certain they killed the marshal."

"Why?"

"They robbed the town of Pleasant," Clint said. "Your marshal tried to muscle in on a share, and they didn't like that."

"Denby did that?"

"Told them we were here, and while your businessman kept us busy, they killed the marshal and left town."

"You're going after them, of course."

"We haven't decided that."

"Why not?"

"Well, for one thing, Sheriff Holliday is out of her jurisdiction."

"Her?"

"Yes," Clint said, "the sheriff is a woman."

"That's ridiculous."

"Well," Clint said, "whatever you think, she's got the badge."

"Look," Mars said, "we need a new lawman. Would you take the job?"

"No, not me," Clint said. "Besides, this is a small town, you don't need a particularly experienced lawman. Your mayor can appoint someone."

"We don't have a mayor," Mars said. "I usually take care of those things."

"Okay, then you appoint someone," Clint said.

"That's what happened with Denby," Mars said. "He was appointed and look how that turned out."

"Well, I'm not available."

"All right, well, what if you and the sheriff bring those men in for murdering the marshal?"

"I told you," Clint said. "She's out of her jurisdiction."

"What about you, then?"

"It's not my business," Clint said.

"Look here," Mars said. "I'm not holding you accountable, even though you killed Jackson at the Ten Gallon—"

"He tried to kill us," Clint said, cutting the man off. "And I held him accountable for that."

"You said the men who killed the marshal robbed a town," Mars said. "Aren't you going to continue to go after them for that?"

"I'm leaving that decision to Sheriff Holliday," Clint said. "And she'll decide in the morning."

"You can't just ride in here and leave us with two dead bodies."

"We're responsible for one," Clint said, "and I've explained that situation. Now, if you don't mind, I've got to get some sleep."

"Will you be leaving town in the morning?" Mars asked.

"Yes."

"Can we talk again before you go?"

Clint heaved a heavy sigh.

"We'll be having breakfast before we go," Clint said.

"There's a café down the street called Lolly's. She has good breakfasts."

"Then that's where we'll be before we leave town," Clint said.

"All right," Mars said. "I'll stop in and talk to you then. Maybe I can convince your lady sheriff to do something."

"You're welcome to try," Clint said. "Good-night, Mr. Mars."

"Good-night, Mr. Adams."

Clint watched Tom Mars leave the hotel before turning and going back upstairs.

Chapter Twenty-One

Although they had taken two rooms, they only used one all night—one room, one bed.

When Clint got back to the room and climbed back into bed with Delores, he told her about his conversation with Tom Mars, head of the Town Council.

"So he expects us to track them down because they shot the marshal?"

"He'd like us to do that," Clint said. "I don't know what he expects. We'll be seeing him at breakfast to tell him what we've decided."

"We're not supposed to be thinking about that now," she pointed out, reaching beneath the sheet.

As her hand closed over his cock, he found it very easy to stop thinking about anything else . . .

***

In the morning while they dressed, Clint was very aware of how quiet Delores was being.

"Are you all right?" he asked.

"I'm fine," she said.

"You're not sorry about what we did last night, are you?" he asked. "Because if I took advantage—"

"Don't be silly," she said, cutting him off. "If anything, I took advantage of you. No, I'm still thinking about what to do next."

"Well, you're right about one thing," Clint said.

"What's that?"

"You have no authority."

"I know," she said. "That's my main concern."

Clint thought her main concern should have been possibly getting killed if she pursued Collins and his men. If she decided to do that, he didn't know if he would be able to let her go on her own. But the job of sheriff was important to her, so he didn't want to do or say anything to influence her decision.

"I'm hungry," she said.

"So am I," he said. "Let's get some breakfast and hope we can eat it before Mars shows up."

***

Tom Mars knew that Medicine Bow was a nothing little town. That was probably the reason the three outlaws had chosen to come there in the first place. And they encountered two men—Jackson and Denby—who had no qualms about bending or breaking the law themselves. Now all five men were gone and the more he thought about it, the more he realized that the town had lost nothing. The Ten Gallon Saloon was still open and running which would probably remain so. Marshal Denby would not be hard to replace, as he wasn't much of a lawman in the first place.

Mars even thought about forgetting about meeting with Adams and the lady sheriff at breakfast, and just letting them leave town. However, Clint Adams *was* the Gunsmith, and it wouldn't do to treat him with any degree of disrespect.

Mars saw Adams and the sheriff enter Lolly's, and decided to give them time to finish their breakfast before he followed them in.

***

Clint and Delores ordered ham-and-eggs with biscuits, and thoroughly enjoyed the meal. Even the coffee was just as Clint liked it, black and strong.

"What a shame a place like this is in a little nothing town like Medicine Bow," Delores said. "I wish it was in Pleasant."

"Have you decided what you're going to do?" Clint asked.

"Yes," she said, "I'm heading back to Pleasant. I'll talk to Mayor Westin, tell him what happened, and see if he fires me."

"Without that fifty-thousand dollars," Clint said, "there might not even be a town, anymore."

"If that happens, I'll just have to deal with it," she said. "After all, it'll be his fault, not mine."

"That's true."

"And maybe Lawrence Crandall will step in and pick up the pieces," she offered.

"I suppose that could happen," Clint said, although after having met Crandall, he didn't think the old rancher would be interested in starting over.

They finished their breakfast and were having a last cup of coffee when Tom Mars entered the café.

"Mr. Mars meet Sheriff Holliday," Clint said.

"Sheriff," Mars said, removing his hat, "a pleasure. I hope you both enjoyed your breakfast."

"We did," Delores said.

"And have you decided what you're going to do?" he asked.

Clint left it to Delores to reply.

"We'll be leaving town and heading back to Pleasant," she said. "I'm sorry, but I have no authority to pursue these men. I'm sorry about your marshal."

"That's quite all right," Mars said. "I actually understand your decision, Sheriff. Thank you both for speaking with me."

Mars turned and walked out, leaving Clint and Delores surprised that he hadn't tried to get them to change their minds.

They paid their bill and went to the livery to pick up their horses.

Chapter Twenty-Two

Clint decided to ride back to Pleasant with Delores. From there he'd decide what his next move would be.

As they entered town, people stopped on the street to watch them ride in.

When they got to the livery, they dismounted.

"You think they've been told I'll be coming back with the money?" she asked.

"They may not have even been told the money was taken," Clint said. "That's the way I'd play it. Why spread the word when you might actually be bringing it back."

"But I haven't," she said. "What does he tell them now?"

"Well," he said, "that's going to be the mayor's decision, not yours."

They turned their horses over to the hostler, but Clint told him to have the Tobiano ready the next morning.

"You'll be leaving tomorrow?" she asked, as they left the livery.

"Time for me to move on," he said.

"To where?"

"I don't always know."

As they headed back to the center of town so Clint could get a room for the night she said, "I guess I'd better go and talk to the mayor, then."

"Remember," he told her, "none of this is your fault, it's his. Let him deal with it."

"I'll keep that in mind," she said. "Can I see you later?"

"If I'm not in the hotel, I'll be in the Hanging Man."

They separated there, and Sheriff Holliday went to City Hall.

***

"This is not what I wanted to hear, Sheriff," Mayor Westin said.

"I'm sorry, Mr. Mayor," she said, "we didn't expect Benny to get killed like that, or for Collins and his men to kill a town marshal."

"So not only do they have our money, they killed a lawman," Westin said. "And you're all right with that?"

"No, sir," she said, "but I have no authority outside this county, and as it is, I went pretty far without it."

"You had the Gunsmith with you," he said. "You could've tracked them down."

"Who knows how long that would take, and how far we'd have to go. Like I said, I have no authority, and it's really not Clint Adams' business. I'm sorry, sir, but I did all I could do."

"In that case," Westin said, "I'm not sure how much longer you'll be wearing that badge."

"That decision is up to you and the Town Council," she said. "I'll wait to hear your decision."

As Sheriff Holliday left his office, Westin sat down heavily in his chair and covered his face with his hands. With fifty thousand dollars gone from his safe, he doubted he or the town of Pleasant had much of a future. Unless he could figure something out . . .

***

Clint got himself the same room in the hotel, then headed for the Hanging Man Saloon. He had no desire to ever go back to the Moon Shadow.

He was on his second beer when a man in a black suit came through the batwing doors, spotted him and walked over. It was midday, and the place was starting to fill with drinkers and gamblers.

"Are you Mr. Adams?" the man asked.

"I am," Clint said, and then got it. "You're Mayor Westin."

"I am," the mayor said. "Can we talk?"

"Can I buy you a beer, Mayor?"

"A whiskey would be better," the mayor said.

"Whiskey for the Mayor," Clint said to the bartender, then looked at the mayor and asked, "What's on your mind?"

Chapter Twenty-Three

"I want to hire you," Westin said.

"For what?"

"To track down the men who stole our money and bring it back."

"You don't want the men brought back?" Clint asked.

"I want the money more than anything else," Westin said.

"I understood that the stolen money belonged to the people in town," Clint said. "How would you be paying me?"

"Well," Westin said, nervously, "I'd pay you from the money you brought back. How does ten per cent sound?"

"Ten per cent of fifty thousand dollars?"

"Yes."

"But what if I don't bring back the whole fifty?"

"Still ten per cent."

"And what if I spend weeks trying to find them, and I don't bring back any money?"

"Then there won't be a town for me to be mayor of," Westin said.

"I'm afraid I'm not for hire, Mayor," Clint said.

"Another whiskey!" The mayor told the bartender. He tossed it back and then looked at Clint. "Why not?"

"I'm not a bounty hunter," Clint said.

"You went out with Sheriff Holliday to try and find them."

"That was just to help her out," Clint said. "As I'm sure she told you, she decided not to pursue them."

"She did tell me that," Westin said. "I don't understand her decision, and I'll have to decide her future."

"Seems to me her future here is tied up with yours, and everyone else's," Clint said.

"I'm afraid you're right," Westin said. "I don't know what to do."

"Hire somebody else," Clint said.

"What?"

"There are plenty of bounty hunters out there," Clint said. "Hire one or more."

"Would they do it for a percentage?" Westin asked.

"That'd be up to them," Clint said. "Bounty hunters usually collect their money when they bring their prey in, but others might want to be paid first."

"It'll take me some time to find the right one," Westin complained. "That is, unless you know somebody?"

"I might know one or two, but I can't speak for them," Clint said.

"Could you contact them?"

"I'll be leaving town tomorrow," Clint said. "I'll see if I can pass the word along that you're looking."

"How will I know you've done it?" Westin said. "We have no telegraph."

"If I find somebody who's interested," Clint said, "they'll come here and let you know."

"That's if we haven't dried up and blown away before then," the mayor said.

"I hope you don't," Clint said.

"I-I don't know what else to do."

"Maybe you should have a talk with Lawrence Crandall," Clint suggested. "I understand he has some money."

"Crandall!" Westin said. "He's going to be the only one who's happy about all this. No, he and I will never work together."

"Then I don't know what to tell you, Mr. Mayor," Clint said. "You're going to have to deal with your loss."

Westin lowered his voice.

"I have to tell the people what happened," he said.

"You haven't told anyone, yet?"

"The Town Council."

"With that many men aware of the theft, I'm sure it's slipped out to some degree."

"You might be right," Westin said. He glanced around. "I've noticed the looks I've been getting, lately."

Clint had also noticed some of the other patrons giving the mayor hard or sly looks.

"I-uh—better get back to my office. If you change your mind—" He didn't finish the sentence, just turned and left the saloon.

The bartender came over and said to Clint, "The mayor sounds desperate."

"Yes, he does," Clint said.

"Does he really think word hasn't got out about what he did?" The man shook his head and walked down to the other end of the bar to serve some customers.

Clint didn't feel bad for the man. He did, however, feel bad for the town, and for Delores Holliday. But there wasn't much he could do. He felt he had already spent too much of his life tracking thieves and killers, getting very little in return except vengeance, which was satisfying him less and less. And there wasn't even the possibility of that here, since he had no personal stake in the town of Pleasant. As for the lady sheriff, he liked her just fine, but not enough to spend days or weeks or more on the trail with her. He saved that kind of commitment for his oldest friends.

He ordered another beer.

Chapter Twenty-Four

Clint was still in the noisy Hanging Man Saloon, nursing a third beer, when Sheriff Delores Holliday entered. She drew some curious looks as she approached the bar, but most of the people there certainly hadn't heard yet that she'd returned empty-handed. At least, Clint didn't think so.

"A beer for the sheriff," Clint told the bartender.

The man nodded and set it up.

"I heard about your meeting with the mayor," he said.

"How?"

"He was here," Clint said. "I guess after talking to you the only thing he could think to do was try to hire me."

"And what'd you tell him?"

"The truth," Clint said. "I'm no bounty hunter."

"How did he take it?"

"He had a couple of shots of whiskey and left."

"Wonder what he's going to do next?" she asked, picking up her beer. "I mean, other than fire me."

"I suggested if he wanted a bounty hunter that he go ahead and hire one," Clint said.

"Make any suggestions?"

"I told him I might, if I thought of somebody," Clint said. He was thinking of his friend is Las Vegas, New Mexico, John Locke, who was known as The Widow-maker, but Locke liked to get his own jobs. And he might have suggested Gavin Doyle, Lady Gunsmith's father, if he knew where he was. "So far, I haven't. What did you do after leaving his office?"

"I had a long bath, hoping something would occur to me to do with my life right now, but nothing did, so I got dressed and pinned the badge back on."

He thought when she came in that her hair smelled like lilacs.

She looked around the saloon.

"I wonder how much these people know?" she asked.

"The mayor thinks he's kept the missing money quiet," Clint told her, "but the other members of the Town Council know, so I'm sure word's got out to some."

She sipped her beer.

"I also suggested he talk to Crandall, but he'd rather let the town die then do that."

"I can believe it," she said.

"He has other options, if he thinks of them."

"Like what?"

"Hire a new lawman and send him out to find them," Clint said. "He could also hire some mercenaries, but all that hiring would take money."

"Which he doesn't have," she said.

"He offered me a percentage of what I recovered."

"That wouldn't work."

"Why?" he asked.

"Come on," she said, "anybody doing the job for money would recover the fifty thousand and keep going."

That was a pretty cynical outlook, but it sounded right to Clint.

Clint and Holliday suddenly became aware of six men standing behind them, half with holstered pistols, the other half with rifles. They were of varying ages, some looking like ranch hands, and others like store-keepers.

"Sheriff!" one of the youngest called out. "You got a lot of nerve comin' in here."

It suddenly got very quiet in the place. Holliday turned to face the men, while Clint remained leaning on the bar.

"Mr. Stacy," she said, "look at the six of you. I could've used you as a posse, but when I asked you all had reasons not to go."

"Bringin' that money back to town was your job, not ours," Stacy said. The other men nodded.

"And what's on your mind now?" she asked.

"We want that badge," Stacy said.

"What are you going to do with it?" she asked. "Which one of you is going to pin it on?"

"That ain't the point," Stacy said.

"What is the point?" she asked.

"That you shouldn't be wearin' it."

The men behind him all nodded.

"Well," she said, "you're all armed; I guess if you want to take it away from me you can."

Stacy licked his lips.

"It'd be better if you just handed it over."

"Oh, I'm sure it would be," she said, "but I'm not going to do that. So the next move is yours."

If possible, it got even quieter in the room, so that everyone heard Clint speak.

"If you gents," he said, eyeing them in the mirror behind the bar, "make me put my beer down and turn around, some of you won't walk out of here. Is that what you want?"

The six men all exchanged glances and looked nervous.

"W-we ain't challengin' you, Mr. Adams," Stacy said. "We don't want no truck with the Gunsmith."

"Well you're interfering with me having a drink with the sheriff," Clint said, "so you've got it. Make up your minds."

One-by-one the men peeled off and left the saloon, eventually leaving the man named Stacy alone.

"Anything else, Mr. Stacy?" Holliday asked.

"This ain't over," the man snapped, and left.

Holliday turned to the bar and gave her attention to her beer.

"Think it's over?" she asked.

"Maybe not," he said, and they drank.

***

Clint spent the night with Sheriff Holliday in his room, as spending the night in one of her cells wouldn't have been convenient.

They woke lying pressed together in bed and Delores reluctantly disentangled herself from him.

"I have to thank you for everything you've done," she said, while they got dressed. "And I mean . . . everything."

"I just wish I could've helped you more in trying to keep your job," he said. Although he didn't think losing the badge would be such a bad thing, but he didn't say so. Better to keep that opinion to himself.

"I'm going to leave you an address where you can reach me," he said. "Let me know what happens."

"I will," she promised, and they left the hotel together.

Chapter Twenty-Five

Two months later . . .

Clint was in Las Vegas, New Mexico, staying with his friend John Locke for a few days. It gave him and the Tobiano some time to rest.

They were standing at the corral, watching the Tobiano among several other horses Locke had at the time.

"You find a new hand?" Clint asked.

"Not so far," Locke said. "I've been workin' the place alone for a few weeks. But I've got some prospects."

Locke usually liked to employ one man to watch his place whenever he went off on a hunt.

"Did you ever hear from that mayor from Pleasant, Wyoming?" Clint asked.

"I did, but like you thought, I wasn't interested in the job."

"Not even for ten per cent of fifty thousand?"

"I thought about that the same way you did," Locke said. "By the time anybody catches up to those three men, that fifty thousand is gonna be a lot less, if not gone. Not worth the effort."

"I figured."

"How about goin' into town to get some supper?" Locke asked.

"Suits me," Clint said, "but can I borrow a horse? I want to let Toby rest."

"Come on," Locke said, "we'll saddle two in the barn."

***

Locke took Clint to a steakhouse that had recently opened in Las Vegas, New Mexico, a town that had started growing.

"Not bad, huh?" Locke asked, as they each worked on their steak.

"Pretty good, actually," Clint said. "Cooked right, and the vegetables are done to a turn."

They each had a large mug of beer to wash it all down with.

"Where are you headed after you leave here?" Locke asked.

"I'm not sure," Clint said.

"Nobody's reachin' out to you, these days?" Locke knew that Clint had a hard time turning down pleas for help, if they came from a friend.

"Not lately," Clint said. "The last person was the lady sheriff."

"Ah, the one from Pleasant."

Clint nodded.

"Sheriff Delores Holliday."

"You said she wasn't qualified," Locke reminded him.

"She was a teacher, until they took that away from her," Clint said. "Then she picked up the badge. She *could* be good at it. She's got the moxie, but she's going to need more experience."

"You think she's still a sheriff there?"

"I'm not even sure there's a town there, anymore." Clint said.

"Probably not, from what you told me," Locke said. "There's probably just a lot of dust."

"Which means she can't still be wearing that badge," Clint added.

"Maybe she moved on," Locke said, "got another job teachin' somewhere."

"I hope so," Clint said. "I think that'd be good for her."

They finished their meals and left the steakhouse.

"Wanna stop in the saloon for another beer?" Locke asked.

"Why not? Then we better head back to your place."

Locke had insisted Clint stay with him and not in a hotel. He wanted to give him a room in his house, but since the bunkhouse was empty, Clint insisted on staying there.

But first, the saloon.

Chapter Twenty-Six

Like the steakhouse, the Rising Sun Saloon was new to Las Vegas. Clint and Locke entered and approached the bar. Several of the patrons greeted Locke by name, most of them just looked over at the two men, knowing who they were and giving them a wide berth. Nobody wanted to get on the wrong side of the Widowmaker and the Gunsmith.

"Two beers," Locke told the bartender.

"Comin' up," the small man said. He set them on the bar. "There ya go, Mr. Locke."

"Thanks."

Locke handed Clint a beer and they both drank.

"This is why I don't come to town that often," Locke said, looking around. "I don't like bein' the center of attention."

"It may not be you they're looking at, John," Clint said.

"I think they're lookin' at both of us, Clint," Locke said. "This is why I have to hire another man, so I can send him in whenever I need supplies."

"Well then, let's finish these drinks and head back to the ranch."

"Just what I was thinkin'," Locke said.

They finished their beers and turned to leave, but at that moment someone came through the batwing doors that made Clint stop in his tracks.

"Well . . ." Locke said.

The woman saw Clint and walked up to him.

"Clint," she said.

"Sheriff Holliday," Clint said. "Meet John Locke."

"Mr. Locke," Delores Holliday said. "A pleasure to meet you."

"The pleasure is all mine, Ma'am," Locke said. He wore a headband rather than a hat, or he would have tipped it.

"What brings you to Las Vegas?" Clint asked.

"I wanted to talk to you in person," she said. "Can we sit?"

"Well, we were just headed out—" Clint started.

"Why don't you stay and talk to the lady," Locke said. "I'll see you out at the ranch."

"Thank you, Mr. Locke," Delores said.

"My pleasure again, Ma'am," Locke said, and left.

The saloon was busy, but there was no music and they'd be able to talk, so Clint said, "Drink?"

"I'll have a beer."

Clint bought two more beers and then they walked to a table.

"How did you know I'd be here?" Clint asked, as they sat.

"Well, you gave me the address so I could telegraph if I needed to, but I wanted to do this in person. I've been here a few days, hoping you'd show up. If not, today I was going to go talk to your friend Locke and see if he knew where you were. But here you are."

Clint squinted at the tin on her chest.

"Is that the same badge?"

"Kind of," she said. "Same place, different name, so different badge."

"The town's not called Pleasant, anymore?"

"Nope," she said, "and everybody isn't smiling. Mayor Westin's gone, and Mr. Crandall's buying back his ranch bit-by-bit."

"I didn't think he'd be interested," Clint said.

"Well, he is, and he backed me to stay as sheriff."

"Got a new mayor?"

"We do, but he's working for Crandall."

"And that's okay with you?" Clint asked. "That Crandall runs the town?"

"It's okay with me that we still have a town," she said, "and I still have a job."

"You've come a long way to talk to me, Delores," he said. "What's it about?"

"It's about fifty thousand dollars," she said.

"The same fifty thousand?"

"Yup."

"Don't you think that money's gone by now?" Clint asked.

"Maybe," she said, "but I'd still like to catch the three men who stole it."

"And you'd like me to go with you?"

"Only for two reasons."

"What are they?"

"Well, it was convenient," she said, "I had to pass this way to get where I'm going, so I thought I'd stop."

"And the second?"

"A poker game."

"What poker game?"

"There's this big poker game taking place in a small town here in New Mexico."

"The one in Moriarty?"

"You know about it?"

"I know some of the people playing in it," Clint said. "In fact, I was thinking of riding over there to have a look."

"And play?"

"No," he said, "there's a big buy-in, and I'm a little rusty."

"Ten thousand dollars to play," she said.

"That's it."

"Well, if you remember, Sam Tennant was playing poker in both Pleasant and Medicine Bow."

"So you think he's going to be there?" Clint asked. "That's a big hunch to travel all this way for, Delores."

"I know," she said, "but I had Mr. Crandall send a telegram."

"Moriarty's got a telegraph?"

"They do," she said. "Mr. Crandall got the names of the players."

"Don't tell me Tennant's playing and he used his real name?"

"He's not wanted in New Mexico," she said.

"But you have no jurisdiction in New Mexico."

"I know," she said, "but I figure I'll stop and talk to the sheriff in Moriarty and get him to back my play."

"So you're not asking me to back your play?"

"I told you," she said, "I had to pass this way, so I thought you might want to finish what we started."

"Are you thinking Tennant will tell you where Collins and Selby are?"

"I'm hoping," she said. "What do you say?"

"Well," Clint answered, "why not?"

Chapter Twenty-Seven

"That's a hundred miles from here," Locke said, later.

"I know," Clint said, "but I was thinking of heading in that direction, anyway. Bat and Luke are going to be playing in that game." Bat Masterson and Luke Short were the best poker players Clint knew, and were also close friends of his.

"Still . . . she took a big chance thinkin' you might be here," Locke said. "Don't that sound odd to you?"

"I'm going along, anyway," Clint said, "and see what happens."

"Well, that's up to you," Locke said. "She *is* the most attractive sheriff I've ever seen."

"I asked her to spend the night here on the ranch, if that's all right with you," Clint said.

"That's fine," Locke said. "In the house, or the bunkhouse?"

"I think the bunkhouse would be best," Clint said, "so I can keep an eye on her."

"It would definitely be a good idea," Locke said, "to keep an, uh, eye on her."

They were once again leaning on the corral, watching Clint's Tobiano.

"How's your search for a hand coming?" Clint asked.

"I've got it narrowed down to two men," Locke replied. "I'll probably hire one this week, look him over for a few days, and then I have a job takin' me to San Francisco."

"When I'm done in Moriarty," Clint offered, "I could stop back here, again, and check on him."

"That sounds good," Locke said, "thanks." He straightened. "I've got to go in the house and do some paperwork. It's the part of owning a ranch I'm not fond of."

"I don't blame you."

"Is she gettin' settled in the bunkhouse?"

"She is."

"Then I'll see the two of you in the mornin'," Locke said. "I can do some bacon-and-eggs for breakfast."

"Sounds good," Clint said. "We'll get going right after."

Clint walked back toward the house with Locke, then peeled off and went to the bunkhouse. When he entered, Delores was lying on one of the cots. She sat up.

"Is this okay with your friend, Mr. Locke?" she asked.

"It is."

"Thanks," she said. "My finances are starting to run a bit low after a few nights in the hotel."

"We'll have breakfast here in the morning and then get going."

"I can't tell you how happy I am to find you here," she said. "I was afraid I was going to have to leave without seeing you."

Clint sat on one of the other cots, facing her.

"So Crandall decided to step in, huh?"

"Yes," she said, "he saved the town, and my job. And nobody cared when he replaced Mayor Westin."

"With his own man?"

"And why not?" she said. "He changed the name of the town, again."

"To what?" Clint asked.

She smiled.

"What else?" she asked. "Now it's called Crandall."

"Why doesn't that surprise me?" Clint laughed.

"And he really wants those men found," she said. "He doesn't want people thinking that Crandall, Wyoming is easy pickings for thieves."

"Does he expect you to bring the money back?"

"If I can," she said. "All or any part of it. But he'll be happier if I bring back any or all of the thieves."

"What then?" Clint asked. "Jail?"

"I think he wants to send them to Medicine Bow to answer for killing the marshal," she said. "That means a noose."

"So he's got it all figured out."

She bounced a bit on the cot she was sitting on and said, "These are pretty comfortable for bunkhouse cots."

"I slept all right the last couple of nights."

"Maybe tonight we can see if they're comfortable for other things," she suggested.

He stood up and unstrapped his gunbelt.

"I was thinking the same thing."

Chapter Twenty-Eight

They were able to have sex on one cot, but sleeping called for two separate ones. Clint woke on his back on his bed, with Delores Holliday's head between his legs.

"Sheriff," he said, "am I under arrest?"

She already had his cock rock hard and licked the length of it before answering.

"I'm not sure," she said. "This will take more investigating."

"Well," he said, putting his hands behind his head, "investigate away . . ."

***

The smell of bacon reached them even before they entered the house. Locke had built it himself, and the three-room structure was exactly to his liking. The front included a sofa and chairs, a table and chairs, and a sink and oven against one wall. It was rustic and comfortable. There were two bedrooms, one of which he kept for guests.

He turned from the stove with a pan in hand and said, "You're just in time. How did you two sleep?"

"Just fine," Clint said.

"And I'm starving," Sheriff Delores Holliday said. "Thanks for this, Mr. Locke."

"You've got to call me John, Sheriff."

"All right," she said, "and I'm Delores."

"Here you go, Delores." He put a plate of bacon-and-eggs in front of her and Clint, then got one for himself. He put a pot of coffee and cups on the table, along with a basket of biscuits, before sitting.

"You're going to make some woman very happy one day, John," Delores said.

"Oh, I don't think so," he said.

"And why not?"

"I don't have a lifestyle that a woman would put up with, Delores," he said. "I'm away half the time."

"Some women wouldn't mind that," she said.

"Well, I'll take your word for that," Locke said.

"You two men," she said. "You must have had plenty of women want to marry you in the past."

"Not so many," Clint said.

"Clint's right," Locke said. "We're just not husband material."

"Well, I can't say I'm wife material," she said, "so I guess we're all in the same boat."

"When does this poker game start?" Locke asked Delores.

"Beginning of next week," she said. "That's the only reason I had the time to stop here and look for Clint."

"Seems to me the game will mean a lot to the town," Locke said. "You really think you'll get the local sheriff to help you grab one of the players?"

"I hope so," she said.

"I bet he will," Clint said, "if you wait for Tennant to make his buy-in. They'll have his money on the table, then, and probably keep it if he's arrested."

"That sounds like a plan," she said.

"Clint has always been a man who can come up with a plan," Locke said.

"From what I've heard about you," she said, "you're not so bad yourself."

"My reputation's with a gun," Clint said, "but John Locke, here, he's got a brain."

"Yeah," Locke said, "they don't call me the Widow-maker because I'm smart. And I'm not the one who's considered a living legend, am I?"

"How long have you two known each other?" Delores asked. "You sound like you have a tremendous amount of respect for each other."

"It's been about ten years," Clint said. "Maybe twelve. He was just a youngster."

"And he was already the Gunsmith," Locke said. "Took me under his wing and kept me from gettin' killed more than once."

"And over the years you've returned the favor more than once," Clint said.

While they ate, they continued to regale Delores with stories of their friendship, and then Delores insisted on being allowed to clean up. Clint and Locke went out to the stable to saddle the Tobiano and Delores's mare.

"She's great," Locke said. "I just hope, like you said, she's grown into the job and won't end up gettin' you killed."

"Don't forget," Clint said, "where we're going, Bat and Luke'll be there."

"Well," Locke said, "that's a good thing, anyway. If I didn't have to hire a new hand and then get to San Francisco, I might even come with you."

"You do what you've got to do, John," Clint said. "And like I said, when we're done in Moriarty, I'll stop back here and check on things."

As they walked the horses to the house, the door opened, and Delores stepped out.

"Thank you for breakfast, John," she said.

"Thanks for cleaning up," Locke said.

Clint and Delores saddled up and Locke wished them, "Good luck."

"I don't need luck," Delores said, with a smile, "I've got the legend, remember?"

They turned their horses and rode off.

Chapter Twenty-Nine

Moriarty, New Mexico

Clint and Delores rode in, making their way down an activity-packed main street. There was a banner hanging above that proclaimed this THE MORIARTY POKER TOURNAMENT WEEK.

"This *is* a big event," Delores said.

"Oh yeah," Clint said. "A lot of the major players in the country will be here."

"I wonder if we'll be able to get hotel rooms?" she said.

"We can only try," Clint said. "Maybe we'll end up in a stable."

They reined in their horses in front of the Moriarty House Hotel and went inside.

"Actually," the clerk said, "I have one room because there was a cancellation—but only one room."

"We'll take it," Delores said.

"Er, for both of you?" the clerk asked.

"Yes," Clint said, "we'll, uh, make it work." He signed the register, and the clerk showed his surprise when he read the name.

"Oh, Mr. Adams!" he said. "You, uh, here, for the tournament?"

"Yes," Clint said, "yes, I am."

"Well then," the clerk said, "you get a special room rate."

"Thanks. Key, please? Two of them, if you have an extra."

"Of course. Do you, uh, need help—"

"That's okay," Clint said, "we just have our saddlebags."

They carried their saddlebags and rifles up to the second floor and located their room. It was on the side of the building, overlooking an alley. Once inside, they couldn't hear much of the noise from the street.

"This was a stroke of luck," she said, dropping her things on the bed.

"Yes, it was," he said, doing the same. "Why don't I go take care of the horses?"

"All right," she said, "and I'll find the sheriff's office."

"You don't want me to come with you?" he asked.

"No," she said, "it should be between him and me, peace officer to peace officer."

"Okay," he said, "then maybe I'll see if I can find a couple of my friends who are going to be playing."

"That's a good idea," she said. "Maybe they know Tennant and can point him out. I'm sure I saw him in Pleasant, but I can't be sure I'd recognize him."

"I'll be sure to ask them."

They went back downstairs together and split up outside the hotel.

***

Sheriff Delores Holliday found the sheriff's office and went inside. Two men turned to look at her. One wore a sheriff's badge, and the other the tin of a deputy. The sheriff was in his fifties, while the deputy was a young man.

"Sheriff?" she asked.

"Sheriff Brody," the older man said. "That's me."

"I'm Sheriff Holliday, from Crandall, Wyoming."

"Yer kiddin'," the deputy said, with a big smile. "A woman sheriff?"

She looked at him and said, "That's right," without smiling.

"That's all, Chris," the sheriff said. "Get outside and make your rounds."

"Yessir."

The deputy took another look at Delores, then went out the door.

"Have a seat," the sheriff said, sitting down behind his desk. "What can I do for you, Sheriff?"

"It's kind of a long story," she said, sitting. "If you have the time, I could use your help."

"Well," Brody said, "let me hear it, and then I'll see what I can do."

She started talking . . .

***

Clint found the saloon that was going to be the venue for the poker tournament. It was called The High Spade. Inside he found all the tables and chairs set up for the matches, and the bar still open. He approached the broadly built bartender, whose white apron seemed to go on for miles.

"Help ya?" the bartender said. "If ya wanna sign in, it's that table over there."

"No," Clint said, "I'm not signing in. Can I still get a beer?"

"Sure thing." The man drew a beer and set it down.

Clint turned and looked across the room to where quite a few men were standing in line at a table, waiting to sign in. He wondered if any of them was Sam Tennant. He couldn't tell, of course, but he did see somebody he knew. He took his beer and walked over.

He got there just as the man turned from the table and saw him.

"Well, as I live and breathe," he said, "Clint Adams."

"Hello, Bat," he said to Bat Masterson.

Chapter Thirty

Clint and Bat went to the bar, where Clint bought his friend a beer.

"What brings you here?" Bat asked. "Are you gonna play?"

"No," Clint said, "I'm here looking for a man who's supposed to be playing."

"What's his name?"

"Sam Tennant."

Bat thought a moment, then said, "I don't know 'im. Maybe Luke does."

"Is he here?"

"Not yet," Bat said. "He'll be getting here later today. Why are you lookin' for this fella?"

Clint told Bat about Sheriff Delores Holliday.

"A female sheriff," Bat said. "That's interesting. Where is she?"

"She's talking to the local law, seeing if he'll lend a hand."

"I doubt he'll do anything until the game starts," Bat said. "They're going to want that money on the tables."

"That's what I said," Clint replied.

"Well, look there."

"Where?"

"Across the room," Bat said. "Mr. Hawkes."

"This match is drawing big names," Clint said. "You and Luke, Hawkes . . . all you need is Brett and Bart."

"Those boys are a little busy at the moment," Bat said. "Somethin' to do with their ol' pappy."

Clint looked around.

"Ten tables?"

"At least," Bat said. "Probably no more, not with that buy-in. You know, while you're here you should play. You'd have as much chance of winning as anybody."

"Not against you and Luke."

"You're not afraid of Hawkes?"

Clint made a face.

"I don't go for all that stuff about not counting your money until the game's over," Clint said. "How else are you supposed to know if you're winning or losing?"

"Well," Bat said, "it works for him. Are you at the hotel across the street?"

"Yeah, we are," Clint said. "They had a cancellation."

"I'm down the street," Bat said. "Do you both have the same room?"

"They only had one."

"What's she look like?"

"You'll see," Clint said. "I'll introduce you."

"Well," Bat said, "I've got to go and make sure Luke's got a room. I'll see you later. How about the four of us for supper?"

"Sure," Clint said. "Meet us in our lobby at six."

"Gotcha." Bat slapped Clint on the shoulder and left.

The line at the sign-in desk was getting shorter. Clint wondered if he could get a look at the sheet.

He put his empty mug down and walked across the room. When he got to the table, the man sitting there looked up at him.

"Signing in?" he asked.

"I'm thinking about it," Clint said. "But I'm wondering who I'd be up against, you know?"

"Well," the man said, "pretty much every well-known poker player is here. What's your name?"

"I'm Clint Adams."

"Omigod!" the man said. "The people in charge would be elated if the Gunsmith was in this tournament."

"Well," Clint said, "maybe if I could just have a look at who's signed in . . ."

The man looked around, then said, "I'm not supposed to do this, but seein' as it's you," and turned the sheet around.

Clint did a quick scan of the sheet. Half of the names were illegible, but halfway down the sheet there it was: SAM TENNANT.

"Thanks," he said to the man at the table. "I'm going to give it some thought."

"You can sign up til tomorrow morning," the man said. "We hope you will."

Clint turned and walked away as another group of men approached. He left the saloon and went in search of Delores Holliday.

***

He was on his way to their room to see if she was there, but as he entered the hotel, he saw her in the lobby. She spotted him, and they met in the center.

"What did the sheriff have to say?" Clint asked.

"Just what you expected," she answered. "He won't make a move until after the poker game starts—if then."

"Did he warn you off?"

"Not at all," she said. "He told me if I wanted to try and take Tennant, go ahead and do it."

"Does he know you're not alone?"

She grinned.

"You're my ace-in-the-hole, Mr. Adams!"

Chapter Thirty-One

Clint told Delores that they were going to have supper with Bat Masterson and Luke Short.

"I better go and clean up, then," she said. "Just stay away from the room for about an hour."

"Meet me here in the lobby around five-forty-five. Bat and Luke will be here at six."

"I'll be here," she said. "Will I need a dress?"

"Oh, the badge will do, I think," Clint said, and she laughed.

They separated, to meet back there at five-forty-five.

***

Delores entered the room and removed her hat and gun. Her meeting with the sheriff had gone just as they figured, but the man hadn't laughed at her like most would've.

She used the pitcher-and-basin in the room to clean up, then kind of wished Clint hadn't listened to her and come up to the room.

***

After Delores went up to the second floor, Clint went to the front desk to see if Sam Tennant had registered there. He hadn't.

"How many other hotels in town?" he asked the clerk.

"There's two, but there's also some rooming houses that're givin' rooms to poker players."

"Okay, thanks."

He stepped outside and stopped just in front of the hotel. Moriarty had grown since he'd last seen it, and the poker tournament was probably going to help it grow even more. He could check the other hotels and rooming houses and still not find Sam Tennant. The best thing to do would probably be to wait until the game started. Then they'd find Tennant at one of the poker tables.

There were some chairs in front of the hotel, so he decided to just sit there and wait for Delores to come down, then they could meet Bat and Luke in the lobby. Just in case Tennant wasn't in town alone, it would be good for him to have his two friends watching his and Delores' backs.

***

He was still seated in that chair when Delores appeared at the front door.

"Damn, am I late?" he said.

"No," she replied, "I just thought I'd get a breath of fresh air, and here you are." She grabbed another chair and pulled it over. "I guess we can wait here."

They sat and watched the activity on the street.

"You know, I've never been a poker player," Delores said. "And I sure never thought a whole town would get this excited about a game."

"They're excited about the extra business they'll be getting from all the players."

"Seems to me something like this would also bring pick pockets, thieves and troublemakers to town."

"You're right about that," Clint said. "The sheriff's going to have his hands full, which is probably why he can't help you. What was he like?"

"Old school," she said, "but he surprised me by not being amused by a lady sheriff. There was a young deputy there who was, but the sheriff kicked him out."

"Maybe he just liked you and wants to keep you around," Clint suggested.

"He's a little old for that," she said. "I told you, he's old school."

"You underestimate your appeal," he said, with a smile.

She was about to answer when she saw two men approaching, both wearing dark suits and smiles.

"Clint Adams, you old warhorse," Luke Short said.

Clint stood and shook hands with both men.

Bat Masterson, Luke Short," he said, "meet Sheriff Delores Holliday, from the town of Crandall, Wyoming."

Holliday stood and shook hands with both men.

"It's a pleasure to meet you, Sheriff," the diminutive Luke Short said. Clint always thought Short wore a stovepipe hat to try to increase his height—not that he needed it. His reputation made him large enough, as far as Clint was concerned.

"Are you two ready for supper?" Bat asked.

"I am," Delores said. "I'm starving."

"Luke just checked in, but I've been here long enough to hear about a restaurant that's supposed to be good."

"Well then," Clint said, "lead the way, Mr. Masterson. We're in your hands."

Chapter Thirty-Two

The restaurant was crowded, but Bat seemed to be able to wrangle them a table in the rear of the place just by mentioning his name.

Bat, Luke and Clint caught up on things they'd been doing lately—pretty much gambling for Bat and Luke, and just drifting for Clint.

Then they got to the reason Delores was in Moriarty.

"So you're hoping his buy-in is the money from your town?" Luke Short asked.

"I'm not holding out any hope of getting that money back," she said, "but he and his friends killed a town marshal. Maybe I can find out from him where the other two are—especially Collins. He seemed to be the boss."

"Sounds like the marshal they killed was on the take, though," Bat said.

"That might be," Clint said, "but he was still wearing a badge, and they gunned him down."

"That can't go unpunished," Delores added. "Not if I have anything to say about it."

The fact that she had no jurisdiction in Medicine Bow, Wyoming didn't seem to bother her now as much as it had when they were there.

"Isn't that up to the law in that town?" Short asked.

"The more I think about it," she said, "the more it bothers me that it happened while I was there."

"There was nothing you could've done," Clint told her. "It happened before we knew it."

"I guess I'm wishing I would've pursued them right then and there," she said. "I'm sure any one of you would've done that."

"I've worn plenty of badges in my time," Bat said, "but I didn't usually travel outside my authority. If it means anything to you, Sheriff, I think you did the right thing."

"I agree," Luke Short said.

"Well," she said, "I think I'm trying to do the right thing now."

"You wouldn't even be here if Lawrence Crandall hadn't found out about this poker game," Clint pointed out. "It sounds like maybe he thinks it's the right thing to do."

"He actually wants me to come back with the money," she said. "I think he's going to be disappointed, after all this time."

"That'll be too bad," Clint said. "I hope he continues to back you if that happens."

"I'm thinking if I bring back even one of the men," she said, "or part of the money, he will."

"Well," Bat said, "the whole shooting match starts up tomorrow afternoon. I'm sure you'll be able to find your man then."

"Neither one of you has ever played poker with a fella named Sam Tennant?" Clint asked.

"No," Bat said.

"Not me," Luke said.

"And if I have anything to say about it," Sheriff Holliday said, "you won't."

***

After supper the four of them went over to the High Spade Saloon. It was the last night the saloon would be open to the public. Once the poker tournament started, nobody would be allowed in except those playing or connected to the action.

The place was lively, with music and girls working the floor. The bar was busy, but Clint and Bat were able to elbow room for the four of them and order beers.

"He could be in here," Delores said, turning to look out over the sea of faces.

"I'd know him," Clint said. "I remember he was with Collins the first time I met him, and he filled me in about the town. I paid more attention to his gunhand than his face, but I think I'd remember him."

"Then he'd know you," Bat said. "Maybe even you, Sheriff."

"I don't recall ever seeing him," she said, "but yeah, he might've seen me around town."

"Well then," Luke said, "if he sees you, he might light out or take a shot at you."

"Then it seems to me you two oughtta get out of here," Bat said. "If Luke or I come across him, we'll let you know. Otherwise, you'll find him at his table tomorrow."

"They're probably right," Clint said. "There's no point in taking a chance he'll recognize us."

Delores drank down half her beer and set the mug on the bar. Clint did the same.

"See the two of you tomorrow," Clint said. "We'll need one of you to get us past the front door."

"No problem," Bat said. "We know the fellas who organized this whole shebang. We'll get you in."

"Okay, then," Clint said to Delores, "we might as well get going."

They left the High Spade and stopped just outside.

"What do we do now?" she asked.

"We go back to our hotel and wait til morning," Clint said.

"And do what?" she asked.

He took her arm and said, "We'll think of something."

Chapter Thirty-Three

Clint woke first, so he was able to admire Delores as she slept, naked and on her stomach. The only word he could think of while staring at her nude ass, was "majestic."

She moaned and turned her head, caught him looking at her.

"I thought I could feel your eyes burning into my ass," she said.

"And a fine ass, it is," he said.

"It must be," she said. "You spent quite a lot of time on it last night."

"I was trying to pass the time."

"Well," she said, rolling onto her side, "you did a fine job of it. The lady was very satisfied. Now—" she reached out to glide her fingers over his relaxed cock, "—it's my turn."

Her fingertips very quickly brought his penis to life, and, as it swelled, she began to pay it all the attention she felt it deserved . . .

***

Sam Tennant was looking forward to this day like no other in recent memory.

He'd been playing poker for years, but never before had the money to enter a tournament like this one. And once he, Collins and Selby had split the take from the Pleasant job, he knew what he wanted to use his for.

He woke early the morning the game was supposed to start and hurriedly got dressed. He knew the first card would not be dealt until the afternoon, but he couldn't sleep, so thought he'd get an early start with a big breakfast.

He left his rooming house clad in the new suit he had purchased specifically for this occasion. He preferred to eat his breakfast somewhere in town, alone, rather than with the other boarders. He had only arrived the day before, in time to register, so he still didn't know where the best places in town to eat were. He figured he'd just walk until he came to one that looked good.

He was hoping that when he got to the High Spade and sat at his table, he'd find somebody like Bat Masterson or Luke Short there. Of course, winning the two-hundred-and-fifty-thousand-dollar first prize was his main goal, but he was also looking forward to sitting across from some legends of poker.

This was the day for which he had been honing his poker skills.

***

Clint and Delores chose to eat breakfast at the same restaurant where they'd had supper with Bat and Luke. It was fairly busy, the waiter recognized them from the night before and sat them at a table.

"Will Mr. Masterson be joining you?" he asked.

"It's possible," Clint said, "but let's just figure it'll be the two of us."

"Yes sir," the waiter said, obviously disappointed.

"Why not introduce yourself so he knows he's serving a legend, even if it isn't Bat Masterson?" Delores asked.

"Believe it or not," he said, "I usually like to keep my name to myself."

"I suppose I can understand that," she said. "You don't need people to be taking pot shots at you while you're eating."

"Exactly."

The waiter brought their breakfast and served it without any further comments. Clint went for steak-and-eggs while Delores chose bacon-and-eggs.

"What's your plan once you locate Tennant at his table?" Clint asked. "Are you going to march him out of there at gunpoint?"

"I'm still not sure," she said. "I don't think I'd like to try it without the local sheriff along. With me not having any authority here, I wouldn't expect Tennant to come along quietly."

"What about waiting until the tournament is over?" Clint asked.

"How long will it take?"

"There's no way to tell that," Clint said. "Could go all week."

"I don't want to wait that long," she said. "Besides, if this is really something he's wanted to do for some time, it'll crush him if I take him away from it."

Clint grinned.

"There's a mean steak I've never seen before," he commented.

"Don't you think he deserves it?" she asked.

"Definitely."

"Then that's what I'll do," she said, "walk him out of there at gunpoint, if I have to."

"Just watch out for security," Clint said. "Most of these games usually hire private guards to make sure everything goes smoothly."

"Maybe they'd back me up," she said.

"That's not what they're getting paid for," he said. "You're just going to have to make due with me."

She smiled and said, "I think I can manage that."

Chapter Thirty-Four

The rest of the sign-ups took the morning, and in the afternoon the High Spade Saloon closed to the public so the games could start. All ten tables were full, so if Clint had wanted to sign up, there probably wouldn't have been enough room.

When Clint and Delores got to the High Spade, the front door was locked.

"How are we going to get in?" Delores asked.

At that moment they heard a lock and the door opened.

"I've been watching for you," Bat Masterson said. "Come on in."

They went inside and Bat closed and locked the door. There was one security guard standing inside and Bat said, "Thanks."

"Sure thing, Mr. Masterson," the guard said.

"You can stand at the bar," Bat said. "Once the games start, you'll be able to locate Tennant. Go over to that table and check the sign-in sheet. It'll tell you what table he's at."

"Okay, Bat. Thanks," Clint said.

Bat went to his table. Clint and Delores went to the bar.

"How about a beer, Sheriff?" the bartender asked.

"That sounds good," Delores said.

The barman put two full mugs on the bar for them, then settled down to watch the action.

"All these men here, just to play poker," she said, shaking her head.

"Take a closer look and you'll see a few women, too," Clint said.

"My God, you're right," she said. "Women playing poker."

"How much odder is that than a woman wearing a badge?" he asked. "These days, a woman can pretty much do whatever a man can do."

"I suppose you're right," she said.

He sipped his beer, then put it down.

"Why don't you stay here. I'll go and find out what table Tennant's at. Oh, and I'd put that badge in your pocket so it doesn't attract attention."

"Good idea."

The poker players were too busy getting settled at their tables, introducing themselves to each other and the dealers, to pay any attention to what was happening at the bar, but Delores took off her badge and stuck it in her pocket, anyway.

Clint walked around the outskirts of the tables until he reached his goal.

"Guess you decided not to play," the clerk seated there said. "Too bad."

"Looks like you've got a full house," Clint said. "Mind if I check at that sheet, again? I'm looking for somebody."

"Go ahead."

The tables on the sheet were numbered, and he found Sam Tennant's name listed for table five. Neither Bat, nor Luke, were at that table. Clint didn't recognize the names of the other five players who were there.

"How are the tables numbered?" he asked the clerk. The man pointed.

"That's number one. Which one are you lookin' for?"

"Five."

"Pretty much dead center, then."

That was too bad. Whatever they did, it would attract attention.

"You're going to be short one player in a few minutes," Clint said.

"Well," the clerk said, "somebody's gotta get eliminated first, don't they?"

"You see that lady at the bar?"

"Yep."

"She's a peace officer, about to make an arrest," Clint said. "I'd appreciate if none of your security people got involved."

"I'll pass the word, Mr. Adams."

"Thanks."

Clint made his way back to Delores and picked up his beer.

"Table five," he said. "When they start dealing you can put that badge back on."

"Got it."

A well-dressed man stood up in front of the room and called out, "Are the dealers ready?"

They all nodded.

"Players, are you ready?"

They all answered enthusiastically.

"All right, gents," the man said. "First prize is two hundred-and-fifty-thousand dollars. Good luck! Start dealing!"

Clint heard all the decks being shuffled, and then the dealing started.

"Let's go," he said to Delores.

She took out her badge, pinned it on, and started walking to table five. Clint followed behind her, and as they neared the table, he recognized Tennant from that first night in Pleasant, when he saw him, Selby and Collins standing at the bar.

"Sam Tennant?" Delores said, when they reached the table.

Tennant looked up and said, "Yeah?" before he realized who he was talking to.

"You're under arrest," Sheriff Delores Holliday said.

Chapter Thirty-Five

Tennant stared up at Holliday. Clint thought if he'd had a gun, he would've gone for it, but all the players were required to give up their weapons.

"You got no authority, here," Tennant said.

"You come with me, and we'll go see the local sheriff," she said. "He's got all the authority I need."

Tennant looked around anxiously. The other players were watching, but nobody made a move. Then he looked past Delores and saw Clint.

"Adams!" he blurted.

"Don't make this hard, Tennant," Clint said. "Do what the lady says."

"You're backin' her play?"

"Every step of the way," Clint said.

Tennant looked frustrated at first, and then as if he was about to cry.

"Can'tcha let me play first?" he asked. "I paid ten thousand—"

"That's too bad," Delores said. "You took fifty thousand from the people of Pleasant. How do you think they felt?"

Tennant stood hesitantly, then started walking stiff-legged with Delores right behind him. The well-dressed host approached Clint and asked, "You wouldn't want to replace him, would you, Mr. Adams? On his buy-in?"

Clint considered it, since the buy-in had already been paid, but in the end he said, "Sorry, no."

"Ladies and gentlemen," the man called out, "we are down to fifty-nine players after our first elimination!"

***

Once outside Clint patted Tennant down, just to be sure he was unarmed. It was getting on toward dusk, and foot traffic on the street was next to nothing, with the poker tournament under way.

"Okay, Tennant," Delores said, "where are the other two?"

"W-what other two?"

"You know," Clint said, "Collins and Selby."

"Them?" Tennant asked. "I dunno. We split up months ago."

"When, exactly?" Delores said.

"I dunno, after we split the money."

"You mean after you killed the marshal and left Medicine Bow?" she asked.

"Now wait a minute," Tennant said. "I didn't kill that marshal. That was Collins who done that. And I also didn't steal the money. That was him, too."

"We have it on good authority that you opened the safe," Clint said.

"Well, yeah, but it was Collins who took the money out," Tennant said.

"You were with Collins when he took the money and when he shot the marshal," Clint said. "That makes you as guilty as he is."

"What about Selby?" Tennant demanded. "He did things, too."

"He's just as guilty," Delores said.

"Well . . . well . . . I'll tell ya where they are, but ya gotta let me play. Ya gotta let me go back inside and play. Whataya say?"

"You said you didn't know where they are," Clint said. "Now you're saying you do?"

"I, uh, I can guess," Tennant said. "I mean, I know where they said they was goin'. I just don't know if they're still there now." He looked at Sheriff Holliday. "Whataya say, Sheriff, huh?"

"No deal, Tennant," she said. "I'm taking you to the local sheriff. If you don't tell us what we want to know, you'll be going back to Medicine Bow to take the blame for the marshal's murder all by yourself."

"B-but, but, I didn't—"

"If you do tell us," she went on, "I'll take you back to Crandall to pay for taking the money. It's up to you if you want to do time for robbery or hang for murder. Now let's go!"

***

Sheriff Ted Brody came out of the cell block and hung the keys on the wall peg near his desk.

"I can keep 'im here for you until you're ready to leave," he said. "But I can't charge him because he hasn't done anything hereabouts."

"That's fine," Delores said. "I appreciate it. But I'd like to go and talk to him."

"Go ahead," Brody said. "He's your prisoner."

"Thanks." Delores looked at Clint. "I won't be long." She went into the cell block.

"She must be quite a lady for the Gunsmith to decide to back 'er," Brody said. Delores had introduced them when she and Clint walked in.

"She's trying to live up to the badge," Clint said, "and doing a pretty good job of it, I'd say."

"Kinda hard for me to accept," Brody said, "women doin' men's jobs, but it's happenin' a lot lately, ain't it?"

"It sure is, Sheriff," Clint said.

***

Sheriff Delores Holliday entered the cell block and stopped at the center of three cells, where Sam Tennant sat on a thin cot.

"Well, Tennant?" she asked. "Have you made up your mind what you want to do?"

Looking very unhappy, Sam Tennant said, "Yea, Sheriff, I made up my mind."

"And?"

"I'll tell ya where Collins and Selby were goin'," he said, "but like I told ya, I don't know if that's where they still are."

"It'll be close enough," she said. "Start talking."

"Selby said he was takin' his share and goin' to Kansas City. Said he was gonna try livin' the city life for a while. Said he might even keep goin' til he gets to St. Louis."

"And Collins?"

"Ol' Mexico."

"Where in Mexico?"

"He said he'd been to some border towns, but he wanted to see real Mexico, so he might go to Mexico City." Tennant shrugged, with his head hanging down.

"That's all I know." He looked up at her. "You gonna take me back to Pleasant now?"

"We'll see," she said and left the cell block.

Chapter Thirty-Six

Clint and Delores ate supper at the same restaurant, which was empty now because the tournament was going on.

"I guess I didn't think this through," she said, shaking her head.

Clint cut into his steak as he asked, "You can't always figure everything."

"One in Missouri and one in Mexico," she said. "What do I do? Go there? Leave Tennant here? Take him back, first? Or just forget the other two, now that I have him."

"Kansas City's not at the other end of the world," he said. "At least it's in this country."

"What if he went to St. Louis?"

"Once you're in Kansas City, St. Louis is easy."

"Have you been there?" she asked.

"I've been to both."

"Have you been to Mexico?"

"Many times."

She poked at her steak with her knife.

"Mexico City?" she asked.

"Yes."

"How far is it?"

He looked across the table at her.

"It's far."

She dropped her knife and fork and sat back in her chair exasperated.

"Do you think Sheriff Brody would hold Tennant while I go off . . . gallivanting?"

"Probably not."

"I don't think so either," she said.

"I have an idea," he said.

She sat forward quickly.

"What is it?" she asked.

"If you start to eat, I'll tell you."

She looked down at her plate.

"I *am* hungry," she said, and picked up her utensils.

"Okay," he said, "Collins, Selby and Tennant, they're all guilty of murdering a peace officer in the eyes of the law."

"Right," she said. "So?"

"So we turn him over to the feds," he said. "We get a federal marshal to take him off your hands."

"Denby wasn't federal, he was a town marshal," Delores pointed out.

"I know," he said, "but the federal government doesn't like when peace officers are killed, federal or otherwise. They'll take him and extradite him back to Wyoming for you."

"Are you sure?"

"I can send some telegrams and find out," he said, "but yeah, I'm pretty sure."

"That would leave me free to go to Missouri."

"Yes, it would."

She hesitated, then asked, "Would you come with me?"

Now it was Clint's turn to hesitate.

"Let me think about that for a while," he said, finally.

"Sure," she said, "of course. I know it's a lot to ask—"

"I'll send the telegrams tomorrow, and by the time we get a reply, I'll decide. How's that?"

"That's fine," she said. "That's all I can ask."

They both turned their attention to their steaks, alone with their own thoughts.

***

After supper they discussed going back to the High Spade, but there was no point. The games were going on, and they had no reason to be there. So instead, they went back to their hotel room.

Clint was already thinking about Delores' request for him to go with her to Kansas City, and maybe St. Louis.

He could do that easily enough, but after that she was sure to ask him to go to Mexico with her, if she decided to go.

That would be a whole other matter.

Chapter Thirty-Seven

The next morning Clint left the room before Delores and went to the telegraph office. It was new, smelling of fresh wood. It had been erected because of the poker tournament.

Clint sent a telegram to U.S. Marshal Bill Vail, in Denver, requesting that Deputy Marshal Custis Long be dispatched to Moriarty, New Mexico to pick up a prisoner who had killed a marshal in Medicine Bow, Wyoming. He sent the name of the town in case, at the other end, they wanted to confirm the event. Hopefully, he'd get a quick reply. Long—known as Longarm—was a friend as well as a U.S. Marshal.

He went back to the hotel to get Delores and go to breakfast. When he got there, however, Sheriff Brody was in the lobby.

"I was just going to go up to Sheriff Holliday's room," Brody said, "but maybe I better talk to you."

"About what?"

"Her prisoner," Brody said. "Seems my deputy was talkin' to some people, and word got back to the mayor about her. He ain't happy."

"What's his beef?" Clint asked.

"That she disrupted the poker tournament, which is important to the town."

"Nothing was disrupted," Clint said. "It went off without a hitch."

"Still," Brody said, "she walked a man out of the High Spade at gunpoint."

"Who said that?" Clint asked. "No guns were used. We walked him out nice and peaceable."

"Well," Brody said, "Mayor Scott wants the man released."

"You tell your mayor if that man is released, somebody's going to get killed. That'll really disrupt the town."

"The town, maybe," Brody said, "but not the game."

"If you let him out of his cell, he'll try to get back in the game."

"So?"

"So in these kinds of tournaments, once you're out, you're out. If your mayor wants to see something interfere with the poker, just let Tennant out, Sheriff."

Brody firmed his jaw and thought for a minute.

"How long do you think she's gonna want me to keep 'im?" he asked.

"I just sent a telegram to get a U.S. Marshal here to pick him up," Clint told the lawman. "That'll probably take a few days."

"U.S. Marshal?"

"Then we'll get Tennant extradited nice and legal," Clint said. "Try that on your mayor and see if it satisfies him. If it doesn't, ask him if he wants to talk to me."

"I don't think talkin' to the Gunsmith is high on his list," Brody said. "That might just shut him up."

Brody left the lobby and Clint went upstairs to tell Delores he had sent his telegram and talked with the sheriff.

"About what?" she asked.

"Seems the mayor's nervous about having a poker player in jail."

"You think I should go and talk to him?"

"No," Clint said, "I sent him a message with the sheriff that'll give him something to occupy his time for a while."

"I hope so," she said. "You think the mayor will object if we get a U.S. Marshal in here?"

"He might squawk a bit," Clint said, "but I don't think he'll object."

They went to breakfast and didn't discuss any options over the meal, because they didn't have many. If Clint couldn't get a U.S. Marshal to come and pick up Tennant, Delores Holliday didn't know what she was going to do.

***

After the meal Clint and Delores returned to the hotel and found a telegram waiting at the front desk.

"What's it say?" she asked, anxiously.

"They're sending a deputy U.S Marshal," Clint said. "He should be here in two days." It wasn't Custis Long they were sending, but it was a deputy, and that's what counted. Clint folded the telegram and stuck it in his pocket.

"We better go and tell Sheriff Brody so he can tell the mayor," Clint said. "Then the rest is up to you, Delores."

***

Sheriff Brody looked up from his desk as Clint and Delores entered. There was also a young deputy standing next to the desk.

"We've got news," Clint said, and handed Brody the telegram.

Brody read it and handed it back.

"Looks like you got your way," he said. "I'll let the mayor know I'm holding a prisoner for federal extradition."

170

"Wow," the deputy said.

"Go do your rounds," Brody told him.

"Yessir." The young man tipped his hat to Delores. "Nice to see you, ma'am."

"That's Sheriff, to you," Brody snapped.

"Yessir," he said to Brody, then "Sorry, Sheriff," to Delores.

"Somebody pull some strings?" Brody asked, handing the telegram back.

"I just asked a question and got an answer," Clint said.

"So will you be waitin' for him to get here, or ridin' out?" Brody asked.

"That'll be up to the Sheriff, here," Clint said. "As soon as she makes up her mind."

"I'll be heading for Kansas City tomorrow," Delores spoke up. "I'm hoping Clint will come along."

"Well," Brody said, "you can depend on me to turn your prisoner over. I don't like anybody who kills peace officers."

"That's good to hear," Clint said.

As he and Delores started for the door, Sheriff Brody asked, "What if your deputy marshal asks me about evidence?"

"Tell him there's a deathbed statement," Clint said. "The marshal told both me and Sheriff Holliday that this man and his two partners shot him."

"That'll do it, then," Brody said. "Can't say as I'm sorry to see you go, Adams. There's enough dynamite in the High Spade without adding the kind of heat you bring. No offense."

"None taken," Clint said, and he and Sheriff Holliday left the office.

Chapter Thirty-Eight

Outside the office Clint said, "So you've decided."

"Yes," she said, "I think I've got to see this through. Now all I need is for you to decide."

"I can do Kansas City," he said. "We'll have to see about Mexico, though."

"We can cross that border when we come to it," she said. "I think I better go and buy some supplies."

"Okay," Clint said, "I'm going over to the High Spade and see if I can say goodbye to Bat and Luke without disrupting the game."

"I'll see you at the hotel."

They split up . . .

***

When Clint got to the High Spade, he found the front doors locked. He knocked, just to see what would happen, and the same security guard from the day before opened the door.

"Oh, hey, Mr. Adams," he said. "You wanna come in?"

"Just for a minute."

"Sure thing."

Clint entered and the security guard closed and locked the door. Looking around, Clint could see the games were underway. There was an empty seat here and there, but for the most part there was still a full complement of players.

He walked to the bar.

"Beer, Mr. Adams?" the bartender asked.

"Sure," Clint said, "I'll do just one."

He didn't want to attract the attention of Bat or Luke, he just waited until they saw him on their own. Every player was allowed a short break, so Bat announced his, and Luke followed. They joined Clint at the bar.

"Do you need help?" Bat asked.

Clint knew if he said yes both men would walk away from the tables and their ten thousand dollar buy-ins to assist him.

"No," Clint said, "we pretty much got what we wanted, so we'll be riding out tomorrow."

Quickly, he explained to them about the deputy U.S. Marshal who was riding in.

"Looking for one man in Kansas City or St. Louis is gonna be like looking for a needle in a haystack," Luke predicted.

"Well, he drinks," Clint said.

"Don't we all?" Bat asked.

"We'll check the saloons and hotels and see what happens," Clint said.

"And then what?" Bat asked. "Mexico?"

"I don't know about that," Clint said.

"Hopefully, we'll be seein' you somewhere down the line," Luke said, shaking Clint's hand and returning to his table.

"You're going to be watching her back," Bat said, "but who's watching yours?"

"I am," Clint said.

"She wears her gun very well," Bat said, "but can she use it?"

"The one time it came up, she didn't hesitate," Clint said.

"Did she hit what she shot at?"

Actually, in that saloon in Medicine Bow with all the tables being turned over, he didn't think Delores had fired a shot.

"We're going to find out," he said, shaking Bat's hand. "I'll see you soon."

"After this I'll be in Denver for a while," Bat said.

"I'll remember that."

He watched his friend walk back to his table, where he seemed to be the one with all the chips in front of him. A glance over at Luke's table showed the same result. He was willing to bet his two friends would end up seated across from each other at the final table. He wished he could see it.

Chapter Thirty-Nine

Kansas City, Ks.

After a last short visit to the cell block, Tennant gave Delores one more piece of information. Pete Selby had often mentioned the city of Wyandotte, Kansas, which was part of "old" Kansas City. That was going to make it easier to find him, rather than having to look all through "new" Kansas City, which was a combination of the old and new.

They rode in and found a bustling city. It had taken two weeks of riding and camping out, so they decided the first thing they would do was get hotel rooms. In the Mayflower Hotel Clint asked for two rooms, and Delores didn't complain. After all that time together on the trail, they would both enjoy some time alone.

They took their saddlebags and rifles up to their rooms, and then Clint left to board the horses in a nearby livery stable.

Delores sat in her room, depressed and concerned that Pete Selby had plenty of time to have been in Kansas City, and left. If they had to try and catch him in St. Louis, it was just going to get harder and harder. She was starting to wonder if any of this had been a good idea. Granted, they had managed to catch one of the three thieves, but they hadn't recovered any of the money. Not that she had expected to, but there had been a germ of hope in the back of her head, and that germ was slowly dying.

She didn't know how much further she would be able to get Clint to go with her after Kansas City, and she wasn't all that sure she wanted to continue on, alone.

***

The longer they spent on the trail, the more Clint could feel Delores' enthusiasm waning. As he left the horses at the livery and walked back to the hotel, he wondered how much longer she was going to be able to keep going? He had the feeling as long as Collins stayed south of the border, the man was going to be pretty safe.

At the hotel he knocked on her door and when she answered he asked, "Ready to get something to eat?"

"I am," she said, looking at him, "but you're going to need to clean those hands."

He looked down at his hands and saw how grimy they were.

"Come inside," she said. "There's plenty of water, here."

The hotel did not have modern amenities. But she was right, there were a couple of pitchers full, and more than one basin, so he didn't have to wash in the same water she'd used.

"How are the streets?" she asked, as she watched.

"Crowded," he said. "This is a busy city."

"That's going to make it harder," she said.

He dried his hands and said, "Let's eat and worry about that later. It looks like they have a full-service restaurant downstairs."

"That suits me," she said. "I'm not in the mood for crowded streets. I've never been a city girl."

They went down to the busy lobby and from there into the connected dining room. Many of the tables were taken, but they managed to find a table for two in the back, as that was usually the last place most people wanted to sit. For people with Clint's reputation, it was the only place.

When the waiter came over, Clint asked, "What's good?"

"We got nice deep bowls of beef stew, with soft, fresh rolls."

Clint looked at Delores and she nodded, so he said, "We'll take two."

"Yessir!" The waiter noticed the badge on Delores' shirt as he turned to leave.

"Is that for real?" he asked her.

"Yes," she said, "but it's from Wyoming."

"That's no never mind," he said. "we give peace officers a discount. We appreciate what you folks do."

"Well," she said, "thanks very much."

"Are you a peace officer, sir?" he asked.

"No," he said, "I'm just along for the ride."

The waiter nodded and headed back to the kitchen. When he returned and set their bowls down in front of them, they saw how right he was. They were very deep, and the rolls perfectly soaked up the gravy.

"I suggest we start with saloons tonight," Clint said, "and move onto hotels in the morning."

"Fine with me."

"Maybe we'll find him drunk or sleeping."

She nodded, not reacting to his joke.

"Delores . . ."

"Huh?" She snapped to and looked at him.

"You should make it an early night. I'll check on some of the saloons."

"No," she said, "you shouldn't do it alone. It's not your job."

"It's not as if I'm going to arrest him," Clint said. "If I see him, I'll just let you know, and you can take it from there."

The Lady Sheriff

In the end they agreed, and, after dessert, she went to her room, and he went saloon hopping.

Chapter Forty

Clint assumed a man with thousands of dollars burning holes in his pockets would want to drink in higher class saloons, so he avoided the smaller places.

He had been to Kansas City before, but not for some time. One of the largest saloons in town had been the Silver Slipper, and it was still there, so that was where he started.

The place hadn't changed since he was last there, still had high crystal chandelier ceilings and a dark mahogany bar. He could see that most of the clientele had money. They were well-dressed and groomed.

"Welcome, sir," the bartender said. "What'll ya have?"

"A beer, thanks."

"Just get to town?" the man asked, as he set the beer down.

"That's right. Actually, maybe you can help me. I'm looking for a man."

"Are you the law?" The bartender seemed to get tense.

"No," Clint said, "but I'm riding with a peace officer."

The man relaxed.

"So who you lookin' for?"

"A killer named Pete Selby."

The bartender thought about it a moment, then shook his head.

"He's got money, and he likes to drink," Clint said. "He's tall, dark-haired, thirties—"

"Look around. All of that matches a lot of men," the bartender said.

"I can see that. Does the name sound familiar?"

"No, sorry." Somebody at the other end of the bar called him. "Gotta go to work."

"Sure."

Clint stayed long enough to drink his beer and check out some of the men standing near him at the bar and sitting nearby at tables. Before leaving, he decided to talk to one of the girls working the floor.

"Selby?" the pretty brunette in her thirties repeated. "No, I don't know 'im."

"What about a dark-haired man in his thirties flashing a lot of money?"

"We have a few of those," she said, "but I know them. They're regulars."

"Excuse me, but regulars meaning how long, exactly?"

"Oh . . . years," she said. "They come in all the time and try to impress me or one of the other girls with their money."

"I see," he said. "Okay, thanks."

"So, what about you, handsome?" she asked.

"What do you mean?"

"Do you have money?"

"Hardly any," he said.

She made a sad face.

"Too bad."

She turned with a wave and went back to her job.

Clint left to check some other saloons before going back to his hotel.

***

"She's right," Delores said the next morning, over breakfast. "There are going to be a lot of men who fit that description."

"So we'll just keep looking," he said. "We didn't come all this way for nothing."

"Clint—"

"Don't say it!" Clint cut her off. "I know you're having doubts, and that's natural. But we're here, so I suggest we just keep moving forward."

She nodded and said, "Agreed!"

***

"Another one," Pete Selby said.

"This early in the day?" the bartender asked. "Are you sure?"

Selby took a sheath of paper money from his pocket and slapped it down on the bar.

"You want some of this or should I spend it somewhere else?" he asked.

"No," the bartender said, "I'll take it." He poured another whiskey for Selby.

"Damn right!" Selby picked up the glass. "I always wanted to have enough money to be an upper class drunk, and now I sure as hell do."

"If that's what you want, I guess you got it," the bartender said.

"Now move on down the bar and serve somebody else," Selby said.

"Sure."

"And leave the bottle!"

The bartender took his hand off the bottle and went to the other end of the bar.

Selby sipped his whiskey happily.

Chapter Forty-One

Clint and Delores made the rounds of saloons the next day, first asking for Selby by name, then describing him. They kept getting the same reaction: lots of men match that description.

Over a beer on their fifth stop, Delores said, "It's too bad there's nothing about this Selby that stands out."

"Like a scar or a missing arm," Clint said.

"Exactly."

"I guess maybe we better start looking at hotels after this."

"There must be more hotels and rooming houses than there are saloons," Delores complained.

"You're probably right. Let's finish up here and get started."

***

Selby saw Clint Adams and the lady sheriff in the fourth saloon they tried that day. Lucky for him he saw them before they saw him. And he was just drunk enough to want to do something about it.

He trailed them to their fifth stop, took up a position across the street to wait for them to come out. There were plenty of people on the street, so that once he fired his gun, he'd be able to blend into the crowd. He didn't know for sure if they were looking for him, but why else would they be in Kansas City, checking saloons? Coincidence? Not a chance. That lady sheriff must' still be searching for that stolen money.

She wasn't going to find it.

***

As Clint and Delores left the saloon, the batwing doors had not stopped swinging when Clint heard the shot, Delores flew back through the doors, into the saloon, and fell to the floor.

Clint looked across the crowded street. He had two choices. He could run across and try to find the shooter or go back into the saloon to see how Delores was. He chose the latter and rushed back into the saloon.

Delores was on her back with a spreading red stain on her chest.

"Delores," he called out, kneeling next to her, "can you hear me? Hang on!"

"Let me by!" somebody yelled to the gathering crowd around them, "I'm a doctor."

Clint looked up, saw a portly man push through the onlookers and crouch down on the other side of Delores.

"This looks bad," he said to Clint. "I need some rags--lots of rags. We've got to stop this bleeding."

Several men broke from the group, ran to the bar and came back with varying degrees of clean and dirty rags. The doctor didn't seem to care, as long as they soaked up the blood.

"We need to get her to the hospital," the doctor said. "Go out and get a buggy, a buckboard, anything we can use to transport her. Hurry!"

Clint hated to leave her, but he stood and rushed outside to do as the doctor said . . .

***

Pete Selby cursed his blurry, drunken vision.

He had been aiming for the Gunsmith and instead, hit the lady sheriff. That meant he was going to have to try again, he thought, as he started running from the scene.

When he was sober . . .

***

Delores was still alive when they got her to the hospital.

As they wheeled her in, the doctor remained outside.

"Aren't you going with her?" Clint asked.

"I've done what I can, Mister," the doctor said. "The rest is up to them."

"Okay, thanks," Clint said, and rushed inside.

He was sitting on a bench, waiting to hear how Delores was doing, when a man wearing a three-piece suit came in, followed by two uniformed policemen—one young, one middle-aged—from Kansas City's modern police department.

They went to the reception desk, talked to a nurse, then turned and came to Clint.

"You were at the shooting at the Julep Saloon?" the suited man asked.

"That's right."

"What's your name, sir?"

"Clint Adams."

The man looked surprised, as did the two officers.

"Well," the man said, "I guess that explains a lot."

"Does it?"

"My name is Lieutenant Fletcher." He was in his forties, tall, the kind of man who wore his authority well. "Care to tell us what happened?"

"It's simple," Clint said. "We were leaving the saloon, and somebody shot her."

"Were they aiming at her, or you, Mr. Adams?" the Lieutenant asked.

"That's a good question," Clint said. "The lady is a peace officer, Lieutenant, a sheriff from Wyoming, so it could've been either one of us."

"A lady sheriff?" Lt. Fletcher said. "What are you two doing in Kansas City?"

"Tracking a killer."

"Looks like he found you."

"That," Clint said, "is exactly what it looks like."

Chapter Forty-Two

Clint was surprised when the Lieutenant sat down next to him on the bench and dismissed his two men. He had expected them to take him to their police station.

"So you think he spotted you and decided to try to take care of you," Fletcher said.

"There's always the chance someone just recognized me and decided to take a shot," Clint said, "but I don't think that's the case here."

"So what's your plan now?"

"Well," Clint said, "I could keep looking for him or just wait for him to try again."

"And you think he will?"

"I think he'd rather do that than start running," Clint said.

"You mean you want him to try again?"

"Yes, I do."

"So you gonna make it easy for him?"

"As easy as I can," Clint admitted.

"And then you'll kill him."

"That'll be up to him," Clint said. "I'd prefer to take him alive so he can pay for what he did."

"Robbery, and murder, you said," Fletcher commented.

"That's right."

"I have to take your word for it."

"Not really," Clint said. "Send a telegram to Marshal Bill Vail, in Denver. He'll back my story."

"I'll do that," Fletcher said. "You know, I've read books about you."

"Don't believe everything you read."

"I usually just believe what I see," the Lieutenant said.

"Good," Clint said, "I suggest you read Mark Twain or Edgar Allan Poe instead of dime novels."

Fletcher smiled. "I'm pretty sure I can do both." He stood up. "I hope your friend is all right. I'm going to leave one of my men here to take a statement from her, when she's ready."

"When she's ready?"

"I like to think positively," Fletcher said. "We'll talk again, soon." He turned and left the hospital.

***

Clint sat there for three more hours before a doctor came out to talk to him. He stood up as the white-coated, white-haired man approached him.

"How is she, Doc?"

"We got the bullet out, and stopped the bleeding," the doctor said, "but it did a lot of damage."

"So is she going to make it?"

"We're going to have to wait and see."

"Is she awake?" Clint asked.

"That's what the policeman asked me," the doctor said. "Not yet. But he's going to stay around to see if—and when—she does."

"If?"

"We don't know just how bad the damage is, sir," the doctor said. "We're going to have to wait to find out. Meanwhile, we're just trying to keep her breathing."

"Okay," Clint said. "Thank you, Doctor."

The man nodded, turned and went back down the hall.

***

Pete Selby waited outside the hospital. It didn't take a genius to figure that was where they would take the sheriff, and that Clint Adams would be there, too. He could even see Adams through the front door each time it opened and closed.

This time he was waiting in a doorway across the street with a rifle. He wasn't going to make the same mistake again. This time he wouldn't miss.

***

Clint sat in the hospital a bit longer, waiting to see if Delores would open her eyes. They allowed him to walk back to the room where she was lying, the policeman sitting by her bed.

"I'm Clint Adams," he said.

"I know, sir," the policeman said. "I was told you might be here."

"Has she opened her eyes?"

"Not yet."

From what Clint could see, her breathing was even and measured.

"You should go back to your hotel, sir," the young officer said. "The doctor said she might not open her eyes until tomorrow."

Clint stared down at her pale face.

"It should've been me," he said.

"Maybe she's lucky it wasn't, sir."

"What do you mean?"

"Now she has you to avenge her."

"That doesn't sound like what a policeman should say," Clint said.

"I guess not."

"I won't tell if you don't," Clint said.

The policeman smiled and said, "Deal."

Chapter Forty-Three

Clint was reluctant to leave the hospital until Delores woke up, but if the doctor was right, he would be there all night.

He told the policeman what hotel he would be in and headed for the door. When he got to it, he stopped. If he was Pete Selby, he'd figure on the hospital and be waiting outside.

He turned and went to the older nurse at reception.

"Is there another way out of here?"

"There's a back door, and a side door," she said.

"Can you show me the side door?"

"Sure, come on."

He followed her, and she led him to the door.

"It leads to an alley they sometimes bring patients in from," she said.

"Thank you."

He went out, found the alley empty at the moment. He worked his way to the front and peered out at the street. People were coming and going from and to their business, or their homes. He looked across the street, picked out some likely vantage points that he would have picked if he was waiting for somebody to come out the front door.

He moved his eyes from one doorway to the next. Two that he picked were shops that were still open for business, so a man wouldn't be able to hide there. A third doorway led to a store that was closed. If Pete Selby was waiting for him, he was probably waiting there. He watched a while longer, finally saw some movement, and the barrel of a rifle.

He stepped from the alley and headed the other way, away from the hospital's front entrance. After he'd gone a few hundred feet, he crossed the street and doubled back. He was sure Selby had his eyes trained on the front door and wouldn't see him coming from one side.

As he got closer to the doorway he slowed down, kept his back to the window of the closed store. A few people walking by gave him curious looks, but nobody said anything.

When he got to within arm's reach of the doorway he waited patiently. At one point the door to the hospital opened, and as if readying himself to fire, the barrel of Selby's rifle came out far enough for Clint to grab it tightly. He stepped away from the window and yanked on it, pulling Selby out of the doorway.

The man came staggering out, saw Clint, and released the rifle. As his eyes went wide, he grabbed for the gun on his hip.

"Don't!" Clint shouted, but it was no use. Selby was panicked, and Clint had no choice. He drew and fired, hitting the man in the chest. Now people on the street noticed, and scattered, ducking for cover.

Clint rushed to where Selby was lying, his pistol on the ground next to him. He kicked the gun away and leaned over the man.

"Where's Collins?" he asked.

Selby just stared up at him.

"Is he in Mexico City?"

"D-d-doctor—" Selby stammered.

"You don't need a doctor," Clint said. "You're going to die, Selby. Tell me where Collins is so he doesn't get away scott free."

Selby's face was etched with pain, and then it went slack as his eyes closed.

"Stop right there!" Clint heard. He turned his head, saw the policeman who had been sitting at Delores' door. The man was pointing a gun at him.

"Take it easy," Clint said, showing his hands. "This is the man who shot Sheriff Holliday, and he just tried to shoot me."

Suddenly, the man recognized him.

"Mr. Adams."

"I'm going to stand up, now," Clint said, still holding his hands out to show they were empty.

"I'm sorry, sir," the policeman said, putting his gun away. "Somebody came running to tell me there was shooting out here."

"One shot," Clint said. "That's all. He's dead."

The policeman walked to Selby, took a look at him and said, "Yessir, he's dead."

"You better send for your Lieutenant, and then we can wrap this up."

"Yessir," the policeman said. "Right away."

***

Clint was back on the bench in the hospital. Selby's body had been removed from the street, and Lieutenant Fletcher was sitting next to Clint.

"So I guess that's it," Fletcher said. "He tried again, and you got him."

"That's right."

"You were lucky to spot him."

"I figured he'd be somewhere out there," Clint said. "I made a point of spotting him."

"We're checking his pockets now," Fletcher said. "Hopefully, we can find out where he was staying, and maybe recover some of that money for Sheriff Holliday to return to her town."

"That would be good," Clint said. "If she survives."

"Oh," Fletcher said, "I meant to tell you. The doctor says she's awake . . .

Chapter Forty-Four

Mexico City

Delores Holliday opened her eyes and spoke to Clint, but the doctor had said there was still no guarantee that she would fully recover.

As Delores looked up at him, he said, "Selby's dead, Delores. He's paid for what he did to you."

Delores stared at him, then her eyes fluttered, but before she fell unconscious again she said, "Collins."

"Don't worry," he said to her, not knowing if she heard him, "I'll get Collins."

He left the next day for Mexico City, and in a month he was there. He realized it had taken him so long to get there that Collins might be gone. But he had promised Delores he would find him, and this was the last place they knew Collins had been.

Clint doubted that the news of Tennant's capture and Selby's death would have reached Collins all the way down here. And if this was the place Collins always wanted to go when he had the money for it, he would still be there, enjoying it.

Clint rode down *Paseo de la Reforma*, so named by President Benito Juarez after French Emperor Maximilian was driven out of power. Clint suspected that a man like Collins would want to establish himself somewhere on Mexico City's main street.

But he turned off the Paseo to find himself a hotel and livery. He didn't want to take a chance of being seen until he was rested and ready.

He found a small hotel that looked like a good place to stop, and a few doors down a livery stable.

"Do you have a room available?" he asked the bored looking desk clerk.

"Señor," the clerk said, "here we always have rooms. He grabbed a key. "*Tres.*"

"Room three," Clint said, accepting the key. "Right. Do you, uh, want to know how long I'll be staying?"

"*Señor,*" the clerk said, "you can stay as long as you wish."

"Uh, the livery down the street . . ."

"They have plenty of room, too."

"Then I'll board my horse and come back."

"As you wish, *Señor.*"

Clint left and walked down the street to the livery. He found a wizened looking little old man who simply nodded when he said he wanted to board his horse.

"I'm staying at the hotel down the street."

"*Si, Señor.*"

He went back to the hotel with his saddlebags and rifle and stopped at the desk, again.

"Do you know of a place where *gringos* gather?"

"There are many *gringos* in Mexico City, *Señor*. And many places where they gather. But I have never been to any of those places."

"Okay," Clint said, "are there any other gringos staying at this hotel right now?"

"No, *Señor*. But you will probably find the answers to your questions on *Paseo de la Reforma*."

"Thank you," Clint said, and went up to his room. As he entered, the first thing he noticed was that everything was covered in dust. The sheets on the bed were threadbare, and the lone pillow was flat.

He sat on the bed: the mattress had very little give to it. Halfway through the trip there, he started to wonder if he had done the wrong thing. Now he was thinking maybe he should have stayed in Kansas City until Delores recovered—if she recovered—and then decide together what to do about Collins. But no, he had done the chivalrous thing and promised her he'd get him.

And here he was, over fifteen hundred miles later.

What if Collins wasn't there? Then he had come all this way for nothing. And at this point, he didn't know if Delores was alive or dead.

He decided to at least find out about that.

He went back down to the lobby and asked the clerk, "Where can I send a telegram?"

"*Paseo de la—*"

"*—Reform*," he finished. "Thank you."

He turned and left the hotel.

***

On *Paseo de la Reform* he sent a telegram to the police department in Kansas City, for Lieutenant Fletcher, asking for an update on Sheriff Delores Holliday's condition. He then told the clerk where he was staying and paid him to deliver the reply.

"*Si, Señor,*" the young clerk said.

Clint left the telegraph office, wondering what his next move should be. He decided on the cantina right across the street. He entered, found many of the tables occupied, but enough empty so that he had his choice.

"Señor?" a black-haired woman in her forties greeted him with a smile. "You would like to eat?"

"I would love to eat," he said.

"*Bien*," she said. "Please, be seated. What may I bring you?"

"Enchiladas and rice, *por favor*," Clint said.

"Ah, the señor speaks Spanish?"

"*Por favor* is all I know," Clint said, and then quickly added, "Oh, and *cerveza*, please."

"Coming, Señor."

She turned and went to the kitchen.

Chapter Forty-Five

Clint felt more hopeful and human after he finished eating and washed it all down with a second mug of cold beer.

"Another cerveza, *Señor*?" the waitress asked.

"No, I've had enough."

He looked around the place. Since he had entered and sat, more tables had been filled, but he did not see any other *gringos* aside from himself.

"Was it all right?" she asked.

"It was great, thanks," he said, "but do you know of a cantina where I might be able to sit, drink and talk with other gringos?"

"There are many, Señor," she said, "but there is one called *Cantina de las Noches* that you might like."

She gave him directions, and luckily it was only a few streets walking distance.

"My name is Carmelita," she finished. "Come back any time you are hungry, Señor."

"I will," he said, "I promise. Gracias."

"*Por nada*, Señor," she said, and he left.

***

It was not a long walk to Cantina de las Noches. As he entered, it seemed to him that half the patrons were Mexicans and half gringos.

The bartender behind the long bar looked like an American, which suited Clint. If anybody would know about the gringos in Mexico City, he thought it would be a gringo bartender.

"Well, howdy," the bartender said. He appeared to be in his late thirties. "What brings you all the way down here, Mister?"

"I'm looking for a man," Clint said, "an American."

"Lots of us down here," the bartender said. "Came down to help them fight their war, and then had to get jobs so we could stay."

"I hope they appreciate that," Clint said.

"They don't," the bartender said. "They hate every mother's son of us." He put his hand out. "Name's Jess."

"Clint."

"Who's this feller you're lookin' for?" Jess asked.

"A killer," Clint said. "His name's Collins. He shot a marshal in Wyoming, after he stole fifty thousand dollars from another town."

Jess' eyes went wide.

"I heard he was coming this way," Clint said, "but it's taken me a while to get here, so he might be gone."

"Well," Jess said, "I doubt he's in here."

Clint looked around.

"You're right, I don't see him."

"Somebody tell ya he'd be here?"

"No," Clint said, "a lady named Carmelita told me gringos drink here."

"She got that right," Jess said, "but gringos with money, not so much."

"So where do Americans with money drink?" Clint asked.

"A few places," Jess said, "most of them down near the President's Palace."

"Do you know the names of the places?"

"Naw," Jess said, "I don't go over there. Too rich for my blood, Clint, but if you're looking for gringos with money, that's where you gotta go. You'll know the places when you see them."

"Okay," Clint said. "Thanks for the information."

"That was information," Jess said, "now comes the advice. Watch out for President Diaz's *rurales*. They take keepin' the peace down here real serious."

"And Americanos with money," Clint asked, "do they get special treatment?"

"That they do," Jess said. "If you're gonna shoot somebody down here, Mr. Adams, you better be careful about it. Make sure it ain't anybody President Diaz has in his pocket."

"Thanks for the advice, Jess," Clint said, fully aware that he had never given the man his last name.

Chapter Forty-Six

Clint made his way down to the area Jess had told him about and saw what the man meant. Here the cantinas were large, well lit, noisy, and all were in the shadow of the Palace.

There were three of them, and Clint checked them all, but in the end, he decided that the largest one was the most likely. It was called the Crystal Palace Cantina. The name had been used by many saloons in America, which would probably make the gringos feel more at home.

***

He spent three days sitting and waiting, examining the faces of every gringo who came through the doors. The batwings were hung high, so it was impossible to look over them from outside and see who was coming in until they were actually inside.

On the fourth day, he was getting ready to give up when the batwings opened, and Collins came strolling in. He had used some of his money to buy fancy clothes and a neat haircut. He looked like a man with money, and some of the others in the saloon greeted him by name.

There were also two uniformed *rurales* in the cantina, sitting at a table together. Collins walked past them on his way to the bar and greeted them.

When he got to the bar, he slapped a couple of men on the backs and bought them drinks. Collins seemed like a real popular man.

Clint stood up and walked to the bar.

"Hello, Collins," he said.

The man turned and looked at him. When he recognized Clint, he didn't seem all that concerned.

"Adams," he said, "what the hell are you doin' down here?"

"I came to take you back."

"You got no authority here," Collins said. "I don't care if somebody in the states gave you a badge, it's no good down here."

"I don't have a badge."

"So you got nothin'," Collins said. "You want a drink?"

"Not with you," Clint said.

"Who told you I was down here? Tennant or Selby?"

"Selby's dead," Clint said. "Tennant's going to prison."

"And now you want me."

"Yes.

"Well," Collins said, "you'll have to take me, but I don't think my friends will like it very much."

"Friends?"

Collins waved his arms.

"All these people are my friends," Collins said, "including those rurales, over there."

"I don't care," Clint said. "You're coming with me."

"And if I don't go?"

"I'm authorized to use deadly force."

Collins laughed.

"Authorized by who?"

"Sheriff Holliday."

"The lady sheriff?"

"That's right."

Collins laughed.

"She's got no authority down here, either."

"Collins," Clint said, "you seem to think I only want to take you legally."

"If you try it illegally, my friends will stop you," Collins said.

"You think these people are your friends because they let you buy them drinks?"

"That's not the only reason."

"Come on," Clint said, "you don't even know any of their names."

Collins looked around, saw the two rurales, and pointed.

"I know Rafael and Francisco."

Knowing they were being pointed out and discussed, the two men stood and grabbed their rifles.

"That's not going to help you," Clint said, raising his voice so everyone in the quiet cantina could hear him. Then he did something he rarely if ever, did—he announced himself. "The Gunsmith has his own authority. Haven't you heard? I'm a legend."

A murmur went through the crowd, the two *rurales* fidgeted. Clint heard several whispers of "The Gunsmith." For once he was glad of his legend, and that it had reached Mexico City.

"Let's go, Collins," Clint said.

"I ain't ridin' back to the U.S. with you, Adams," Collins said. "You're gonna have to kill me, right here."

"That's really what you want?"

"No," Collins said. "I don't think you're gonna do it with those rurales here."

"You mean those two nervous soldiers with the rifles?" Clint asked.

Collins looked over at the two uniformed men. Clint took the opportunity to draw his gun, take a step, and slam it against the side of Collins' head. He hated to use his gun that way, but one time wasn't going to damage it.

Collins sank to the floor.

Clint holstered his gun and looked over at the two rurales, who both smiled at him, bobbed their heads, and left the saloon. Clint bent and took Collins' gun from his holster. Then he checked the man's pockets and found a handful of Spanish coins. He dropped them onto the bar noisily.

"Drinks for everybody until this is gone," he told the bartender.

"*Gracias, Señor.*"

While everybody ran to the bar, Clint grabbed Collins by the shirt collar and dragged him out.

*** *

Two months later, Clint and Sheriff Delores Holliday rode into the town of Crandall with Collins tied to his horse. Clint had managed to recover some of the money from Collins' hotel room in Mexico City, and then from Selby's room in Kansas City. It wasn't half what had been taken, but it was something. He figured they'd be happy to have some of the money back, and they could do what they wanted with Collins—maybe even turn him over to a federal marshal for the murder of the lawman in Medicine Bowl.

The people of Crandall were happy, as was Lawrence Crandall. Clint waited in a saloon while Delores met with Crandall and the new mayor.

When she walked into the bar, Clint had a beer waiting for her.

"Here's to the sheriff of Crandall, Wyoming," Clint said. "I'll bet they're pretty happy with you."

"So happy," she said, "that they're going to reopen the school."

You mean—"

She nodded.

"I'm taking off the badge and going back to teaching," she said. "At least doing that I'll never get shot again."

"I'll drink to that," Clint said, and they clinked glasses.

Coming March 27, 2021

THE GUNSMITH
468
Death in the Family

**For more information
visit:** www.SpeakingVolumes.us

On Sale Now!

THE GUNSMITH *series*
Books 430 - 466

For more information
visit: www.SpeakingVolumes.us

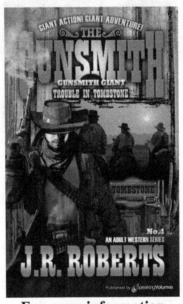

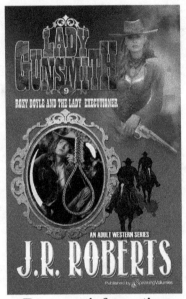

On Sale Now!

Award-Winning Author
Robert J. Randisi (J.R. Roberts)

For more information
visit: www.SpeakingVolumes.us